When I was young, I wanted to be a lawyer when I grew up. But then I changed my mind because being a famous, yet totally undercover secret agent would be much cooler. I looked into it, but there weren't many job opportunities. I thought for a while and concluded that maybe I should just marry well. People make whole careers of that. I fell deeply in love with Agent Mulder, but he already had Scully, and I don't share.

So, instead, I became a writer. Now I get to be all of those things and so many more.

You can follow me on Twitter @LisaFoxRomance.

Her Perfect Lips

LISA FOX

Harper*Impulse* an imprint of
HarperCollins*Publishers* Ltd
1 London Bridge Street
London SE1 9GF

www.harpercollins.co.uk

A Paperback Original 2014

First published in Great Britain in ebook format by Harper*Impulse* 2014

Cover images © Shutterstock.com

Lisa Fox asserts the moral right
to be identified as the author of this work

A catalogue record for this book is
available from the British Library

ISBN: 9780008123246

This novel is entirely a work of fiction.
The names, characters and incidents portrayed in it are
the work of the author's imagination. Any resemblance to
actual persons, living or dead, events or localities is
entirely coincidental.

Automatically produced by Atomik ePublisher from Easypress

To booze, beads, and New Orleans.

Chapter One

Stacy took her usual seat at the long conference table and arranged her notes in front of herself. Her coworkers filed into the large, airy boardroom, cups of coffee, water bottles, and tablets in hand, ready for the monthly All-Staff meeting. She smiled vaguely at them all, tapping her fingernail against the glass tabletop, waiting to begin. These multidepartment progress reports were informative, and very often fun, but her time could be better spent today. There was a mountain of paperwork waiting on her desk and her own part of the meeting was going to be small, she only had one minor update to offer, but it was a positive one. The staff-focused Instagram account she had opened for Sharpe Designs last month was getting some quality followers and loads of great comments. Her goal today was to encourage everyone to keep posting new, amusing pictures. Maybe there was some way she could deliver that message and then sneak out.

She gave Kat Greer a little wave as the stunning blonde graphic designer entered the room. Kat's boyfriend, chief programmer, Dean Kirkwell followed close behind. Stacy made a mental note to grab Dean after the meeting and get an update on the Fisher account he'd been promising her for days. He must've known she was thinking about him because he caught her eye and winked. She smiled back, watching them settle into seats at the back of the boardroom. They were such a gorgeous couple, a perfect picture of contrasts. Kat was a New York goddess in her black Anna Sui dress and Trash and Vaudeville heels, while Dean looked like he had just stepped out of *GQ*, the hottest new face of "urban preppy." But despite the seemingly outward differences, everything about their relationship could be summed up in the way they looked at one another. It was as though they were always sharing a wonderfully secret joke. She envied them a little bit.

The CEO and co-owner of Sharpe Designs, Ron Sharpe, entered the room, and the meeting was quickly called to order. Ron's partner and husband, CFO, Alan Altman, started things off with an announcement that the company was doing better than ever. He explained that they were already outearning their projected figures and this was going to enable them to spend more freely in areas they thought they would have to neglect this financial year.

The lights dimmed for Alan's PowerPoint presentation and Stacy's thoughts drifted as the slides flicked across the screen in a blur of colors and graphs. She really needed to pick up her dry cleaning tonight or the place was probably going to sell all her stuff. She had no excuse for letting it sit there for so long either, the shop was only about two blocks away from her Ludlow Street studio. It wasn't like she had to travel across town or anything. She had a good pile going at home now too, maybe it was time to do a trade. Go to the dry cleaners, pickup and drop off, then grab her tablet and reward herself with dinner at that new little Austrian café on Delancey.

Alan's presentation ended and there was polite applause. Throats were cleared, clothing rustled, people drank water, and checked their phones as the director of development set up his progress report. Stacy shifted in her chair, trying to find a more comfortable position. She glanced at her wristwatch, the clock on the wall, the digital display on her tablet. They all told her the exact same thing. There was a lot of meeting left to go. She shifted again and saw Dean lean over and whisper something into

Kat's ear. From the flush on Kat's cheeks and the side-glance she gave him, it was obvious that whatever he said was definitely not work related. She smiled, happy for them, but her own loneliness made her heart heavy. Here she was thinking about dry cleaning while they were going to go home and have awesome sex. Yay, Friday night.

She rested her chin in her hand and exhaled a long, weary breath. She worked hard at dating, just as hard as she worked at everything else, and in all the time she'd been in New York City, she still hadn't found her 'Mr. Right.' She couldn't figure out what she was doing wrong. She went to the right bars, joined singles groups, had an online dating profile, but nothing ever seemed to work out. There had been a few promising starts, but nothing special. Nothing lasting. And certainly nothing even close to that hit-you-in-the-gut kind of desire she craved. She'd never been a quitter, but the search was taking its toll. She was almost ready to believe it was a lost cause.

"Stacy Saunders!" Ron said, his jovial voice breaking into her melancholy thoughts.

Stacy's heart leapt to her throat and she blinked as she looked around the table, a little disconcerted by all the eyes upon her. Obviously something had happened—something good from the way people were smiling and clapping. She plastered a toothy grin on her face and pretended she knew what was going on.

"As you all know, Stacy has recently been promoted to senior marketing manager," Ron said, addressing the room as a whole.

The staff nodded, some applauded, others shot her smiles.

"What Alan and I didn't tell her," Ron went on, beaming over at her, "was that because of her dedication and hard work, we're also sending her to New Orleans to attend the Advanced Marketing and New Business Innovation Conference."

Stacy's mouth fell open. Surely she had not heard him right. A chance to attend the ultimate rock star conference of the marketing world?

"Come on up here," Ron said, motioning for her to join him at the head of the table.

Stacy rose on trembling legs. She was glad she hadn't worn super high heels today. She might not have made it to the front of the room unscathed. Her heart swelled when the applause started again, and she held her head up high as she made her shaky way to Ron's side.

Ron stood up when she arrived and held out his hand to her. "We know you'll do great things."

She took Ron's hand, stupefied, speechless. She looked at him, at everyone gathered around the table, and she had to bite down on her lower lip to keep from screaming with joy. This was exactly what she had been working toward since the day she took the marketing specialist position with Ron and Alan a few years ago. She had just achieved one of her major professional goals a full two years before she anticipated it would happen. The success felt really good. "Thank you," she said, shaking Ron's hand firmly. "I won't let you down."

With the trip approaching, her first order of business was to hire two new marketing associates to join her team. She needed to get that done before she left. It was a difficult, time-consuming task, and she loved every minute of it. There were hundreds of résumés to review, and she found twelve solid candidates to put through the rounds of interviews. The whole process took longer than she'd hoped, spanning the entire month before the conference, but the new staff were in place when it was time for her to leave for New Orleans.

The journey itself was uneventful, filled with the usual disgruntled travelers and sour security agents, but the minute she stepped out of the airport, and the thick, swampy air coated her skin, her pulse quickened. Some of her favorite memories were of New Orleans and the year she'd spent waiting tables on Bourbon Street after graduating from Loyola. Those had been the best times, a time to be young and free and totally wild. Five years had passed since she landed her first real job and left the French Quarter behind, but being back felt a lot like coming home.

"Welcome to New Orleans," the shuttle driver said as he hoisted her luggage into the back of the van.

Stacy gave him a huge smile in return. "It's great to be here."

The conference hotel was on Canal, on the Quarter side of the street. Check-in took forever, the slow pace of New Orleans never giving way to the impatience of the new arrivals. A water foundation bubbled serenely in the center of the lobby. The Muzak version of "Separate Ways" drifted over from the adjacent bar, accompanied by the clink of glassware and the low, constant hiss of air conditioning. People sighed and shifted their weight, checked their watches, murmured into phones.

After an eternity, she had her key card. She sent her bags off with a bellman and went to go wait on another line for her registration packet. This one moved a tad faster, so after only a single century, she had her badge and materials.

She took the elevator up to the twentieth floor, high above the restaurants and bars and cottages of the Vieux Carre. The room was pretty standard—beige walls, king-sized bed, Degas reproduction, desk, minibar, dresser, nightstand, but it offered a spectacular view of the river. She pressed her fingers to the glass and traced the curve of the mighty, muddy Mississippi until it disappeared into the distance. Stories and stories below her people were drinking and carousing, singing and stripping, making love in the sultry afternoon. Business as usual for the French Quarter.

She dragged herself from the window, sat down on the bed, and opened her packet. Inside were a few sponsor ads, a trade magazine, her credentials, and a hard copy of the agenda she had already downloaded onto her tablet before she'd left New York. She scanned the itinerary again, just in case she'd missed something. She was definitely going to the Brand Growth and Strategy Workshop, and she liked the look of the Global Trends talk. There was nothing on the schedule for tonight though, and the official

Welcome and Opening Remarks Reception wasn't happening until ten o'clock the next morning.

She put the packet aside with a grin. Nothing on the schedule tonight and nothing until late tomorrow morning—that only meant one thing. "Cocktail time!" she announced to the empty room.

Day or night, it was always happy hour somewhere in New Orleans, and the hotel bar was no exception. She arrived on the first floor and found it filled with people, some very obviously for the convention, others just in town for a long vacation weekend. A few attendees even wore their nametags, already advertising themselves and their positions. She wished she'd thought to grab hers. The point of being here was to get her name out there as much as possible.

She spun on her heel, ready to go back upstairs for it, but as she turned, she made eye contact with an average height, darkly blond man across the room. He stood to the left of a group of by the bar, holding a pint of beer. They exchanged a long glance and then a smile. He was probably just a little older than she was, maybe right around thirty, trim enough body, expensive, though not custom-tailored suit. Not bad at all. Maybe her badge wasn't totally necessary right now.

She walked toward the bar, wondering if he'd meet her there, hoping that he would. The purpose of this conference was to meet people after all. A friendly discussion with an attractive colleague seemed like a good way to begin. She gave him another glance over her shoulder and then chose a space where there were a couple of empty stools, a subtle hint and an open invitation.

The bartender took her order for a Cosmo, and Stacy smiled inwardly when she sensed her new friend hovering by her side. She turned to meet his gaze and was pleased to discover that he was as attractive close up as he had been from a distance.

"Hi," he said, holding out his hand to her. "I'm Peter Walker."

He had a deep, if not resonate voice, and no discernable accent.

"Hi," she replied and took his hand. "Stacy Saunders."

"Where are you from, Stacy?" he asked, taking the empty seat beside her.

Yes, come into my lair, she thought with giddy delight. *I have cookies*. He met her gaze and she flashed him a wide smile, trying to cover up her urge to giggle. "I live in New York. I'm the senior marketing manager at a boutique web design firm called Sharpe Designs." Just saying her new title out loud gave her a wonderful little thrill. "Where are you from?"

"Boston," he said, leaning against the bar to signal the bartender. "This conference was part of my promotion package. I'm the vice president of Customer Insights at DataX Ltd."

Stacy waited as the bartender took Peter's order, poured him an Abita Amber, and then hurried off to serve the ever-increasing crowd. "Congratulations," she said, holding out her glass to him. "Promotions make all those long hours worthwhile."

They toasted one another and drank. She sighed contently as the cool liquid slid down her throat. Drinks just tasted better in New Orleans.

Peter placed his beer on the bar and moved a little closer to her. She caught a whiff of his cologne, something spicy and sharp in her nose. "I'm thinking about buying myself a Porsche to celebrate when I get back."

She blinked and gave him a small smile in reply. Something about his admission set her teeth on edge, for no reason. People were entitled to buy nice things for themselves. There was nothing wrong with that.

"I've never been to New Orleans before," he went on, flashing her a winning smile. "I'd like to see some of the city before I leave."

"It's a great city." She took another sip of her cocktail. "I used to live here. I loved it."

"Did you? Why did you leave?"

A spark of interested illuminated his eyes. He was an attractive man. She didn't understand why she wasn't feeling any real connection with him. She wanted to. "This is a great place and I would've loved to stay, but the only industry here is tourism. I wanted my first job to be with a big firm, somewhere where I could interact with a lot of people. I needed to be in New York."

"I understand. My first job was with one of the oldest marketing firms in Boston. Of course, I was recruited during my junior year at Brandeis, but it made sense to stay anyway. I knew even in high school that Boston was where I'd make my mark."

Stacy nodded, not really sure how to respond, or if his statement even required a response at all.

"So, since you lived here, you must know some great places." He touched her wrist, a light brush of his fingertips. "Maybe you can show me around."

He was arrogant for sure, but he was also good-looking and ambitious, a well-dressed companion with a ready smile who would do well at company cocktail parties. Those were definitely good traits in a man. Boston was not all that far from New York. If things worked out, it would be very easy for them to see one another often. They might be able to share a very advantageous partnership and maybe even something more. She met his gaze and gave him a wide smile, open and inviting. She might be able to make this work. "I could do that."

"You know what I'd really like to see?" he asked, leaning closer to her, giving the conversation an air of intimacy.

"No, what?" she asked, doing her part and moving closer to him.

His gaze flicked over her and there was much more than just professional interest in his eyes. "Bourbon Street."

Stacy couldn't help but recoil. "Why?"

He grinned like a little boy. "I hear it's wild."

"It is…something." She took another sip of her drink, trying to think of a way to derail this train of thought. She did not want to deal with Bourbon Street, with the stink and the sordidness, the amateur drunks and assorted vermin. "But there are better things to see in the French Quarter." She flashed him what she hoped was a meaningful look. She'd never really been a very good temptress, but she did try on occasion. "Private courtyards and gardens." She paused for effect. "Dark bars."

He shook his head, oblivious to her attempt at seduction. "Yeah, but Bourbon Street. I don't think I could miss that."

"Hey," a petite, raven-haired woman in a group next to them called over. She was stunning, just one of those perfect women with flawless skin, shiny hair, and deep blue eyes. The sexy girl-next-door fantasy in real life. "Did I hear that you're going to Bourbon Street? We were just talking about walking over. We should all go together!"

"Yes," Peter said, nodding enthusiastically. "That sounds excellent."

The eagerness in Peter's tone made Stacy frown. This was not a positive development. "Super," the woman said. "What are your names?"

Stacy knew everything was lost by the way Peter smiled at their newfound companion. "I'm Peter, and this is Stacy."

"I'm Melanie." She looked to Peter and flashed him a brilliant, white smile. "This is perfect. Going in groups is the best, don't you think?" She turned back to the other people she was with. "Come on everyone, let's go!"

Peter gave Stacy's shoulder a quick squeeze, finished his beer in one gulp, and motioned toward the exit. "After you."

Right now she had a decision to make. She could go along with the group, return to her room and spend the night alone, or try to meet some other people and persuade them not to go to Bourbon Street. She looked at Peter's eager grin and told herself that it wouldn't be too bad. At least it wasn't Mardi Gras or Jazz Fest or even a Saturday night. She could do this. And maybe he was worth it. She gave him a single nod and followed him out of the bar.

The group left the hotel and walked up Canal Street. Two blocks later, they arrived at their destination. Bourbon Street was just as she remembered—loud music and neon lights, frat boys in muscle shirts and girls in crop tops, the stench of beer and pine-scented antiseptic cleaner, the sidewalks littered with garbage and puke. Their little entourage stumbled into the first club they found, which had "Play That Funky Music" blaring from the speakers. Stacy shook her head. Some things truly never changed. Bars on Bourbon Street would play that song until some ultimate, catastrophic apocalypse finally managed to wipe the city out for good.

The barker at the door proudly announced that the club was now offering their world famous three-for-one happy hour. The vodka tonic Stacy ordered was served in a plastic cup the size of which was rarely seen outside of a 7-Eleven. It contained more alcohol than any human should probably ever consume in a single serving, and she was glad to see that in addition to the bad music, the drinking culture had not changed either.

She headed toward the back of the club, outside into the little courtyard area where the music was somewhat blunted and she was less likely to have a drink spilled over her. The others followed, people in the group talking amongst themselves and goggling at the drunken antics on the dance floor. Peter had fallen back to walk alongside Melanie, and they ambled slowly, their heads close together, taking softly. Stacy sighed. So much for the whole reason to participate in this journey. Not that she could blame him. Melanie was gorgeous. Still, the rejection stung. Not that it would've worked anyway. The distance between them would have eventually become a hassle.

She sipped her cocktail, watching the dance floor light up red, then blue, then green as the strobe light pulsed over the dancers. Once again, she had a choice and none of her options were all too appealing. She could go back to the hotel and try to find a new group of people to talk with, she could go to bed, or she could stay right where she was and basically drink alone.

"Let's go someplace quieter," Peter shouted over the music and everybody agreed.

She followed them back out onto Bourbon Street, seriously considering her next move. *Should I stay or should I go now?* She let the chorus play out in her head and in that one millisecond pause, a drunken man wearing only jeans shorts and plastic beads lunged at her from the crowd. She sidestepped around him and almost collided with a woman exiting Pat O'Briens. The woman squealed and Stacy veered off the sidewalk into the street. A group of tourists swept her away, forcing her backward along with them. She fought against the wave of bodies, but it was a losing battle. And then, out of nowhere, a hand grabbed her arm, a lifeline in the storm.

The tourists continued on their journey, but Stacy was held in place, firmly anchored by that strong grip. The hold on her arm was a little too familiar for a stranger and she wasn't sure if she wanted to thank or berate her rescuer. She turned, and her breath caught when she recognized her savior. "Hello, Ten."

"Hey, Stacy."

He grinned and every single part of her tingled. He was as attractive as she remembered—tall and strong, with rich, chocolate-brown hair, and a twinkle of mischief in his startling green eyes. The years had changed him only slightly, taking away the softness of youth and adding hard ridges and planes to his handsome face. His hair was a little too long, and he had a two-day beard, but the scruffiness didn't take away from his almost poetic good looks. And though she would never admit it out loud, just the way his thighs filled out his well-worn blue jeans sent a thread of wicked heat trickling down her spine. Ten was the stuff of all kinds of naughty fantasies, and a few of her favorite ones instantly flashed through her mind.

"There you are," Peter called, cutting through the never-ending stream of people. "We thought we'd lost you."

"Sorry," Stacy said, though she wasn't. She'd forgotten all about him. She gestured toward Ten. "I ran into an old friend."

Peter looked from her to him, back to her. He held out his

hand to Ten. "Hi, I'm Peter Walker."

Ten glanced at her, a million silent questions in his raised eyebrow. Are you with him? Should I step back? Do you want me to get rid of him? She answered them all with a slight shake of her head.

Satisfied, he turned back to Peter with his charming, professional smile, the one that had got him a lot of tips—and even more phone numbers—when they'd worked together. He dropped her arm and took Peter's hand. "Tennyson Landry."

Melanie joined them then, sliding up close to Peter. She was followed by the group, and they created a little cluster in the middle of the street. People flowed around them, to-go cups in hand, beads around their necks.

"It's so good to see you," Stacy said, touching Ten's arm. She couldn't quite believe he was there, but his bicep was hard and firm and very real under her fingertips. "Do you still live here?" She wouldn't be surprised if he had moved. New Orleans was a transient city. People came, hung out for a while, and then left for better jobs, better homes, 'real' lives. Just like she had.

"Yeah," he said, his eyes never leaving hers. "I've got a little place up on Magazine now."

She smiled, ridiculously pleased to see him again. The huge crush she had fostered and fed five years ago had obviously not dwindled over time. He still made her weak in the knees, gave her skin that deliciously tight, tingly feeling. She probably could have spent the entire night grinning up at him like a fool, but Melanie stepped in, standing very close to Ten.

"We wanna go someplace fun," Melanie said, giving him one of her brilliant smiles. "Do you know anywhere good?"

Stacy was about to give Melanie a few key suggestions on where she should go, but Ten put his hand on her shoulder, capturing her attention.

"Let's have a drink," he said, his eyes never leaving Stacy's. "It'll be nice to catch up."

Plastic beads whizzed past her head, crackling on the pavement. A group of men on the balcony above chanted "*Show your tits!*" to a bunch of women below, and every time one of them obliged, they were showered with beads and adoration. Bourbon Street would never change, and she was sick of it already. She nodded to Ten. "Let's go somewhere else."

He took her hand, gave it a gentle tug. "Come on."

She caught Melanie's frown out of the corner of her eye and a little malicious grin curved Stacy's lips. It was probably a character flaw that made her dislike the other woman so much, but she wasn't about to fight that feeling. She laced her fingers through Ten's and let him lead her away from the garish lights and drunken vulgarity.

"What were you doing on Bourbon?" she asked, as they turned onto St. Peter and headed toward the river. No self-respecting local went to Bourbon Street unless they absolutely had to.

He looked over at her, a huge grin on his handsome face. "I could ask you the same thing."

She shook her head, smiling even as he pulled her close to get around a woman puking next to an overflowing garbage can. "I'm just a tourist now, in town for a convention."

He raised an eyebrow, amusement flashing in his eyes. "Is that right? So, what? Are you trying to get sloppy drunk and sleep with the locals?"

She glanced over at him. Well, maybe one local. "That is a solid plan."

He laughed with her as they turned onto Decatur, and then headed back toward Canal. A frenzied Cajun tune blasted out of a souvenir shop on the corner, bright Florissant lights illuminated the sidewalk. "I was just stopping in to see a friend at work. I don't spend much time in the Quarter anymore."

There were so many things she wanted to ask him. What he was doing now, where he was working, what he had been up to for the last five years, but their conversation was cut short when they approached a dark alley, a long corridor tucked between two buildings. Stacy looked around, trying to orientate herself. The fire station was still there like she remembered, and the House of Blues a little farther down, but she had no memory of this place.

"Is this new?" she asked, as he led her down the narrow alleyway.

"Yeah," he said. "It's only been here about a year."

The passage curved and then emptied into a wide courtyard surrounded by brick walls and banana trees. People sat around wrought-iron tables, drinking and laughing. A brass band performed in the corner, playing a low, bluesy tune filled with promise and longing.

Ten headed straight for extensive bar built into the rickety, old building that had probably once been the slave quarters for a house on Decatur. He signaled one of the bartenders, then glanced back at her. "You gotta get an Electroshock."

"A what?" she asked.

He gave her a wicked grin. "Trust me."

She knew that grin too well. This was going to be something dangerous. And probably really fun. She nodded, and he ordered one for her. He handed her a clear plastic glass filled with chartreuse-colored liquid that tasted suspiciously like Kool-Aid.

They meandered over to an empty table in the far back corner of the courtyard. Stacy brushed her damp hair off her forehead as she settled into her chair. She'd forgotten how humid it was here, how her skin was prone to "glisten."

Much to her chagrin, Peter and Melanie found them and sat down without any invitation in the empty seats opposite them. Melanie brushed a lock of hair off her forehead and Stacy noticed with some annoyance that the other woman even made sweating look beautiful.

"Tennyson," Melanie said, favoring him with her beautiful blue-eyed gaze. "What an interesting name. Is it a stage name of some sort?"

He leaned back and extended his arm across the back of Stacy's chair. She was hyperconscious of his arm draped behind her, and the hair on the back of her neck stood up at electric attention. "Oh, no," he said, flashing Melanie that charming smile of his. "My mother's a poet. She teaches at Bennington. I'm just thankful every day that she didn't name me Cummings or Yeats."

Stacy smiled to herself, recalling the night she'd asked him a very similar question. They'd decided to conquer the 'Drink Around the World' challenge at The Alibi to celebrate the completion of her training at the Cabin and they'd just begun a beer from Honduras when the alcohol really started to settle in. He'd told her about his mother and how much she loved the British poet laureate. He claimed to dislike the poet's work himself, yet that didn't stop him from reciting one of his namesake's more famous works, *The Lady of Shallot*, right there among the servers, strippers, and Quarter rats congregating in the bar. He did it with so much gusto, he even earned himself a resounding round of applause.

Melanie nodded like Ten had just told her something profound, and Peter touched her shoulder, trying to regain her attention. Melanie turned back to Peter and Ten caught Stacy's eye, gave her a little wink. She wondered if he remembered that night too, if it left the same kind of impression. They used to have a lot of fun together. No one in her life was quite like him and she missed that. She missed him. New Orleans was an adventure, a fairy tale, and though she loved New York, it was all work and ambition.

Ten picked up his drink and reached over the table to tap his glass against hers. "Welcome back, Prom Dress."

She snorted a laugh and picked up her glass to drink with him. Of all the things for him to remember, it would be that ridiculous nickname.

"Prom Dress?" Melanie asked, fluttering her long lashes at Ten. "Did I hear that right?"

Everything about Melanie rankled. Stacy had no desire to share anything with her. "It's not a very interesting story."

Ten shrugged. "It's probably one of those 'you had to be there' things."

"Oh, come on," Peter said, trying to be a part of the conversation. "Tell it."

Ten looked to her, and after only a second's hesitation, he waved for him to tell it if he wanted to. It was a good memory, embarrassing, but wonderful too. She wanted to share it with him again.

He nodded once, then turned to the group. "Well," he began, "once upon a time, Stacy and I worked at the Creole Cabin Bar and Restaurant on Bourbon Street. This was long before she left for New York City and fame and fortune. Back then, she was humble waitress, a poor college grad just trying to get ahead."

She rolled her eyes, but smiled. Ten loved to tell a good story. He'd often kept the staff entertained even on the slowest shifts.

"She was always running off for interviews, meetings, networking events," he went on. "That day, I think it was an interview with a Google recruiter." He turned to her. "Wasn't it?"

She blinked, shocked that he remembered such an insignificant detail. Shocked and more than a little touched. "Yes, it was."

"Anyway, the Cabin is an extremely loud place. It's right on Bourbon, and all the doors are always open, and they've got this zydeco band playing, people are talking…" He took a moment to meet all of their gazes. "You get the picture."

He took a sip of his drink, then leaned forward, resting his elbows on the table. "It was a hot summer afternoon, the restaurant was dead, the a/c was blasting, but we were all sweating, standing around in the side station talking about nothing 'cause we were so damn bored. Stacy's gathering her things, she was the first one cut, and the other servers and I were a little jealous, so we were kinda ignoring her."

She was there with him again, reliving that day in full color. She could feel the sweat on the back of her neck, the smell of deep-fried shrimp on her skin. She was desperate to get home and take a shower before she went to that interview. That *had to* happen, but it was going to be close. She needed to leave immediately.

"We were used to talking loudly, always screaming at each

other to be heard." He met her eyes, sharing the memory with her. "When it was time for her to go, it only made sense that she would scream good-bye."

He started to laugh, but quickly suppressed it. She wanted to hit him now just as much as she had wanted to back then. It wasn't that funny. "So, she hollers, '*Well, I'm off like a prom dress!*' But at that exact moment, the band decided to take a break." The laugher bubbled out of him, and Stacy winced, just as she had done in that instant, endless moment of silence. "It was just one of those gaps in noise that happens sometimes and everything was quiet at that precise moment. The whole restaurant heard her, the band, the customers, even the guys the kitchen. We all froze, too dumbfounded to move."

He winked at her, but she just shook her head. She had been mortified, every eye in the place on her, her booming announcement seeming to echo in the sudden stillness.

"But Stacy," he said, putting his hand on her knee, "she never blinked. She held her head high and marched right out that restaurant, like it was all perfectly natural. But, boy she did move fast." He met her gaze and lowered his voice an octave. "It must have been quite a prom night." He looked back to the others and grinned. "The name just stuck. It was perfect."

She had to laugh. That restaurant could be such a miserable place sometimes, filled with drunks and non-tipping tourists, but when Ten worked alongside her, she always had a good shift. Some of her best memories were of cackling like a lunatic in the side station with him, making up wild, intricate fantasies about strangling the customers and how they would go about walking out in the middle of a shift in the wake of a boldly delivered righteous tirade.

The music changed, morphing into an upbeat jazzy instrumental tune. Melanie popped up from the table, grabbed Peter, and dragged him toward the forming dance floor. Stacy watched them go, her heart full of old memories, good times and bad.

Ten sat back in his chair and crossed his long legs beneath the table. He rubbed some of the condensation off his glass with his thumb, then licked the liquid off his finger. "So, what's this convention you're in town for?"

He was so damn sexy it hurt. Her crush was back in full force, stronger than ever and full of longing. Every time he met her eyes, her heart beat a little faster, her blood ran a little hotter. She could easily get lost in his gaze, and she had to look away before she could answer. "It's a marketing convention. The 'Advanced Marketing and New Business Innovation Conference' to be precise. It was part of the package I received when they promoted me to senior marketing manager."

He smiled and reached out to stroke her hair. "That's great, Stacy. It's what you always wanted."

His touch sent tingles down her spine and only added to her pride. "Yeah, I'm happy." For some reason, her voice caught on the last word, and she hoped he didn't notice. She *was* happy. She was accomplishing things way ahead of her most ambitious expectations, living the exact life she wanted—for the most part.

He nodded, his eyes never leaving her face. "Are you seeing anyone?"

The question made her skin feel pleasantly tight. "No. Are you?"

Their gazes locked, and he shook his head. The air seemed very warm suddenly, almost too thick to breath. Her eyes dropped to his full lower lip and tension hung between them, heavy with electric promise. "Hey, Ten," a perky young waitress said as she stopped by the table. She pointed to their empty glasses. "Want another?"

He looked to Stacy. "Would you like another?"

She had to take a deep, trembling breath before she could answer him. Wow, that was intense. She was almost glad for the distraction. Another drink sounded nice, but it might be dangerous. She had to stay in control and that was always a difficult thing for her to do around him. Still, one more drink probably wouldn't hurt. "Okay, one more. But that's *it*."

"Uh-huh," he said, flashing the waitress the peace sign. *Two.* "I've heard that before."

Stacy laughed. He had heard it before. Many times, on many nights. And all too often, she was by his side when the sun rose over the Quarter, stumbling home in the glaring light.

It didn't take long for the waitress to return with their cocktails. She collected Ten's money and left with a large smile on her face. He always was a good tipper.

Stacy took a sip of her drink, the sweetness exploding on her tongue. The familiar lightheadedness of intoxication warmed her skull, and she frowned. She might not have the tolerance to take on Mardi Gras anymore, but she was no lightweight either. She held up the plastic cup, the low light reflecting in the funky yellow-green liquid. "What's in these things?"

He gave her that wicked grin again. "Good old-fashioned New Orleans grain alcohol."

Even as her eyes widened, she had to chuckle. No wonder she was feeling it. The drink in her hand was a one hundred and ninety proof bomb of pure alcohol. "Are you trying to get me drunk?"

"Maybe." His gaze moved over her, so slowly and thoroughly it almost felt like a physical caress. "Wasn't that part of your plan?"

Her gaze flicked to his lips and then quickly away. God, she still had it so bad for him. She took a quick sip of her cocktail to try to cool herself down.

He reached over took her hand. "I've thought about you."

Every molecule in the air between them instantly ignited. "Have you?" Heat rushed to her cheeks, her pulse raced in her veins. "What'd you think about?"

He ran his thumb over her knuckles. "Do you remember that night?"

"Of course I remember." She would never forget the night before she left for New York. The night she spent with him. The memory often came to her in the darkest hours, when she was home, alone in her bed. No one had ever held her the way he did, no one's skin had ever felt quite so good against hers. "I almost missed my plane."

He traced patterns over the back her hand with his thumb, a delicate caress that made her blood run hot. When he met her eyes again, tension exploded between them, turning her insides liquid. Her gaze fell back to his lips, and she couldn't help but remember the taste of his kiss. The way he'd touched her. The texture of his skin. Given the chance to have it all again, she'd start right there at his mouth and then work her way down to his—

"Hey," Peter said as he and Melanie returned to the table. "Do you want another drink?"

"No," Stacy said, rising to her feet. This was too much. "I have to get back to the hotel." *And take an ice cold shower.*

Ten stood up as well. "I'll walk with you."

She waved him off. The last thing she needed was Ten anywhere near her hotel room. That was just too much temptation. She wasn't a kid anymore, and she wasn't in New Orleans to get laid. She needed to remember that. "Thanks, but it's just around the corner."

"Stacy," he said, his voice stern, a tone she knew all too well. It was the one he used whenever he thought she was being unreasonable. She'd heard it a lot. "This city is dangerous."

She couldn't really argue with that. He was right. The city was dangerous. And it wasn't smart to walk alone. She knew that all too well. The very first night she moved out of the Loyola dorms and into the Marigny was a night that should have been like any other. But that night, seven murders occurred in a sixteen-hour span. Seven different people were killed for seven different reasons in seven different places all within the city limits. She had missed one of those murders by a single block. If she had turned left instead of right… A graveyard chill raced down her back. It wasn't something she liked to think about. "Okay," she said, and turned to the others. "Do you guys want to walk back with us?"

They wanted to stay, so Stacy and Ten said their goodbyes and exited the bar. They turned onto Canal, and Ten grabbed her around the waist to keep her from colliding with a Lucky Dog vendor heading into the Quarter for his shift. She wrapped her arm around him, enjoying the heat of his body.

"How long are you in town for?" he asked, the weight of his hand on her waist wonderfully distracting.

"Four nights," she said, and ducked as a group of college girls tossed glitter into the air like it was fairy dust. "I leave Monday morning." She brushed the glitter out of her hair, the sparkles raining down on her clothes. "I have the chance to make a really good impression, Ten. This conference is a big deal and there are a lot of people I need to meet. I think, if I can work it right, I might be able to land a speaking role for next year. That would be amazing."

He smiled and hugged her closer. "You haven't changed a bit."

She shrugged. "I know what I want." She glanced up at him. "What's up with you? What are you doing now?"

A man jumped in their path, offering them a pamphlet on how to find Jesus, and Ten waved him away. "I have my own gallery now. I paint. Sell some art. The guy I went to see on Bourbon is an artist I want to work with."

"That's excellent," she said, genuinely pleased, but also a bit surprised. She hadn't thought he'd taken his painting all that seriously. Her impression had been that it was something he did, not anything he'd had plans to do professionally. But then, he hadn't taken very much too seriously back then, he just slid by on a wish and a sexy grin. They were both older now. Maybe he had changed. "I'm happy for you."

"Thanks. It's small, but it does well."

They entered the lobby and headed toward the elevators. Ten pressed the button, and when it arrived, they rode up in silence, sharing the car with a few other conference attendees. She snuck a quick glance at him, the heat of him warming her side. Would he go for the goodnight kiss? Part of her hoped he would, while the other part of her cringed at her lack of self-control.

They exited at her floor and walked side by side down the empty hallway to her room. They paused at her door and Ten touched her shoulder, a light caress that scorched her insides. "Can I take you to dinner tomorrow night?"

"I'd like that," she said before she had a chance to tell herself all the reasons why it would be wrong and unproductive. She wanted to see him again. Her heart demanded this indulgence.

He took a small step closer to her, and she could smell his cologne, a clean brisk scent that made her tummy flutter. "I close the shop around seven. Is eight all right?"

"Perfect." The last meetings of the day would wrap up around five. That would give her plenty of time to get ready. She reached into her pocket for her phone. "Is there a way I can reach you in case something comes up?"

He gave her his number, looking over her shoulder while she punched the information into her contacts. "If I don't hear from you, I'll just assume that we're on."

"Good." She looked up at him, grinning like a teenager. Just being close to him made her feel giddy and vibrantly alive.

He dipped his head and pressed a kiss to the corner of her lips. She'd slept with him, been naked and hot and sweaty with him, but this one, little kiss set her completely on fire. For one second, she thought about inviting him in. But even her most self-indulgent side knew that was not a good idea. She took a step away and placed her hand over his heart. "Goodnight, Ten."

He took her hand and gave it a gentle squeeze. "See you tomorrow, Prom Dress."

She laughed as he walked away, watching him until he disappeared into the elevator. She let herself into her room, tossed the key aside, and went through her usual night routine. Tennyson Landry was not someone she'd ever thought she'd see again. She'd forgotten how good it was to be with him, how just one look could make her feel so beautiful. It had been a long time since she felt beautiful.

She crawled into bed and turned out the light. Tomorrow was going to be a full day. She needed to be rested and alert. She snuggled under the covers and dreamt of times long past, early morning sunlight and the scent of jasmine.

Chapter Two

Ten parked his bike about a half a block up the street from the front of the hotel, away from the confusion of people coming and going, the shuttle vans and cabs, the uniformed bellmen. He looked up at the building and his blood heated, prickling his skin. Stacy was up there, waiting for him.

He stripped off his leather riding gloves and a smile touched his lips as he tucked them into his back pocket. Stacy had intrigued him from the very first day she started at the Cabin. A sassy little redhead fresh out of Catholic college, she was mischievous and intelligent and always up for fun. He'd flirted with her endlessly, but she never took him seriously. Of course, he flirted with everyone, but with her it was always different, a little smarter, a whole lot more sincere. He tried and tried, but she never caught on. Her mind was firmly elsewhere, always looking ahead to the future she had strictly mapped out for herself long before they ever met. She wanted what she wanted, and nothing was going to make her deviate from her plans. Not even him.

But then, on the night of her going away party, her last night in New Orleans, he finally got to be alone with her, finally got to kiss the lips he'd fantasized about for a year. That kiss had blown him completely away. It was the kiss he measured all other kisses by since and none had ever compared.

He could recall every detail of making love to her even though it had been like something out of a dream. And when he'd held later, deep in the night, he was pretty sure he was madly in love with her, but he knew that telling her would be a colossal mistake. *"I've wanted this for a long time,"* he'd said instead, but he thought maybe she understood what he really meant, that maybe she felt it too. For one single second, the look on her face was so raw, so real, he thought they might have a chance. That maybe she wouldn't leave after all. Maybe she would be his. In that one instant, he would have ripped his heart from his chest with his bare hands and given it her if she asked.

Ten sighed, the pain in his chest as real as it had been all those years ago. She'd held his gaze and then squashed his delusions the very next moment when she shook her head and turned away. He was crushed, but he understood. It was never meant to be. From the day he'd met her, she'd been preparing to leave. But that night, that one night, she was all his. They made love one more time before dawn, a long, slow goodbye, and then she was gone, off to New York and the future she wanted.

A horn blared and Ten jumped, rudely dropped back in the present. He shook his head and let out an embarrassed snort-laugh. There he was standing in the middle of sidewalk like some gobsmacked fool, gaping up at the hotel like a crazy freak. Thank God he was in New Orleans. In any other city, he'd probably be arrested.

He circled the bike and took the bouquet of flowers he'd picked out for her from the saddlebag. It had taken him almost twenty minutes to get the arrangement right, the perfect balance of roses, baby's breath, and lace. He fluffed the cellophane, examining the buds for any damage during transit. The velvety petals tickled his fingertips, soft and delicate. He hoped she liked them. He wanted to make her smile. He liked it when she smiled. He always had.

He entered the hotel and crossed the lobby to the elevators, his body humming with barely suppressed excitement. After their first and last night together, he never thought he'd ever see her again. Her ambition had always been clear and staying in New Orleans was never part of her plans. When she left, he had accepted that it was forever. And it still was, he reminded himself as he approached her room. Nothing had changed. She was only in town for a convention. She was going to leave in a few days.

He knocked on her door, his pulse racing. He needed to get a grip. He was acting like a little kid. This was not his first date. But he couldn't stop the heat from rocketing through his veins when she answered the door.

"Hi," she said. Her dark eyes flicked to the flowers, then back to him. "Are those for me?"

"Yes." He held them out to her and was rewarded with the smile he had hoped for. Every bit of effort was worth that.

"Thank you." She opened the door wide. "Come in."

She turned, and his breath caught, the sway of her hips as she crossed the room making his throat go dry. Her vibrant red hair was piled high on her head in a messy bun and fine tendrils curled around her ears, down the back of her neck. If there was ever a more beautiful woman, he'd be hard-pressed to name her.

"What should I put them in?" she asked, but didn't wait for him to respond. She grabbed the ice bucket off the dresser and then went into the bathroom.

He heard the faucets turn on, and he looked around the room while he waited for her to reemerge. The bed dominated the space, a massive king-sized monstrosity, which he could all too easily picture them getting lost in for hours.

She carried the bucket out the bathroom, placed the arrangement next to the TV, and held up her hands like she was Vanna White showing off a letter on the Wheel of Fortune. "How do they look?"

"Fantastic," he said, and they both knew he wasn't talking about the flowers. He took her in, absorbing every detail. Her lips were red and glossy, plump and ripe. The urge to taste them again was a physical ache. His gaze flicked to the bed and then quickly away. It was time to go. He cleared his throat, slamming a lid down on the heat that just wanted to rise and rise, and cocked his thumb over his shoulder toward the door. "Are you hungry?"

"Starving," she said, and headed for the exit. "Where are we going?"

He offered her his elbow, and she slid her arm through his, her hand resting on his bicep. Her scent filled his head, different than what she used to wear. This was lighter, sweeter. He liked it. "The Garden District." He escorted her down the hall. "To a somewhat new restaurant named Blanchard's."

She smiled at him as they entered the elevator. "What kind of food do they serve?"

"Basic New Orleans fine dining," he said as they passed through the lobby. "The usual Creole-French-Cajun fusion."

"So, gumbo, bisque, blackened, brûlée?"

He laughed. "Exactly."

They exited the hotel and strolled up Canal Street. As usual, the night was warm and humid. People in various stages of drunkenness loitered on the sidewalk, a ragtag preacher stood on the corner, megaphone in one hand, pamphlets in the other, while teenagers lingered in front of Popeye's fried chicken. When they arrived at his bike, he reached into the saddlebags and grabbed the spare helmet he'd brought for her.

"Nice bike." The way she caressed the black leather seat gave him all kinds of pleasant ideas. "Is this new?"

"No, it's actually quite old. It's a 1947 Knucklehead."

She playfully poked him in the side. "I know that. I meant, did you buy it recently?"

"I picked it up about three years ago. It was really nothing more than just a frame then. It's been a pain to get parts, she's worth it."

"You built this?"

"Well, rebuilt." He ran his fingers over the chrome handlebars. "It's an eternal work in progress."

She smiled. "The best things always are."

He didn't think she knew how right she was. He handed her the helmet and for the first he considered what she was wearing. He liked the sight of her bare legs, long and lean, smooth and white, the curve of her ankles and her low-heeled sandals, but that short skirt was probably not the best riding attire. "I think you might want to change."

"And miss out on you looking at my legs like that?" She grinned and shook her head, holding his gaze.

Ten laughed. She was so damn bold. It made flirting with her so much fun. He very deliberately dropped his gaze back to her legs, slowly tracing the line of muscle in her calf and thigh. He followed the line higher, imaging the rest of the journey, all that was still hidden from his eyes. "The road can be rough."

She swung her leg over the back of his bike, settled on the seat, and tucked her skirt under herself. She held his gaze as she parted her legs so he could sit between her thighs. "I can handle a little rough."

Ten laughed to himself as he climbed onto the bike. She was going to be the death of him. Her bare legs bracketed his and he ran his fingers down her length of her thigh, pausing at her knee. "We'll go nice and slow."

"I like slow too," she said and wound her arms around his waist.

He was very conscious of her behind him, her thighs gripping him, her body pressed against his, hugging him tight. The air was sweet as they left the Quarter behind, heavy with the scents of fresh rain, plants and earth and growing things. It combined with her perfume, making him giddy, dizzy. There wasn't a lot of traffic heading uptown, so he was able to keep the speed down and they enjoyed a nice, easy ride.

He pulled into the tiny alley beside his place, next to the florist shop where he had bought her bouquet. They dismounted, he stowed the helmets, and led her around the front. The gallery was a small two story bit of post-Katrina new construction that the German artist he'd bought it from had painted sky-blue, a bright and cheery color that stood out and yet oddly blended with the Greek Revivals and shotgun houses, the high-end salons and fashionable restaurants. He waved to the building and the old-fashioned wooden signpost displaying the name, *Gallery 2609*. "This is my place."

Her eyes gleamed in the soft twilight. "Can we go look?"

"Of course," he said, privately thrilled that she wanted to see his work. He wanted to share it with her, to please her with it. He wanted her to like it. His gaze flicked up to the second floor, to his bedroom, and then quickly away. He really needed to get ahold of himself. "Let's eat first."

He escorted her across the street, his arm around her waist, the curve of her hip under his palm. She was gorgeous, the most beautiful woman on the entire street, and he was proud to be by her side. She might be leaving in a few days, but tonight she was all his.

Patrick, the chef-owner, greeted them warmly at the door and showed them to a semi-private table in the far back corner of the courtyard. Ten held out a chair for her and she sat with her back to a brick wall, framed by creeping vines and fragrant pink blossoms. The colors complimented the blush on her cheeks, the hue of her hair. She was a painting, an abstract in bold, sophisticated color and black. He wanted to capture her beauty, capture this moment, and maybe paint it later.

"Come here often?" she asked, flashing him another incredible smile.

One smile and he was ready to fall to his knees and promise her anything. Did she know what kind of effect she had on him? He didn't think so. And it was probably better that way. He smiled in return and handed her a menu. "It's across the street from my place, and Magazine has become a collective of sorts. We send a lot of business each other's way."

They reviewed their choices in comfortable silence. Ambient

jazz music played from speakers subtly placed along the edge of the courtyard. Ten was very aware of the touch of her knee against his under the table, the heat of her body through his jeans. Their waiter arrived and he forced himself to concentrate on ordering. They settled on seven different dishes, a gluttonous array of appetizers and entrees, complimented by a highly recommended bottle of rosé.

She took a long drink of wine, smiled, and settled back in her chair. "You have to tell me how you came to be a gallery owner."

"Well, you know how things go down here. I kinda fell into it. I left the Cabin about six months after you did and started bartending at The Audubon."

Her eyebrows shot up on her forehead and she laughed. "That crazy old bar on St. Charles? Wasn't it a hotel or something?"

He nodded. "Yeah, at one time. The upstairs was all boarded-up—really haunted and creepy. It probably should've been condemned years ago. We only used the bottom floor, which was more than enough. It was a warren of former guest rooms and offices, most of them empty and completely falling apart." He snapped his fingers, a sudden recollection making him grin. "Do you remember that 'art show' we went to there? *Live art* they called it. We had to tour through the rooms, each one with a different, freaky installation. I had nightmares about that skinny guy in the tub of black paint for weeks." He laughed. "That place was so insane."

She shimmed her shoulders in an exaggerated shiver. "I just remember how dark it was. Naked light bulbs, lots of shadowy corridors, people in black eyeliner." She moved closer to him and her perfume filled his head, mixing with the magnolia, made him dizzy. "I can't believe you worked there."

That had been such a different time in his life, when he had been trying to figure out who he was, what he wanted. "Me either, but I really needed a change from Bourbon Street, and it was all local."

She nodded, placing her hand over his. "I get that."

He didn't need to explain to her how hard it was to work on Bourbon, how burnt out a person could get. She knew. "Anyway, I met this artist from Berlin there, a regular customer— he drank Malört all night, every night." Ten's own stomach clenched at the thought. "I don't know how he did it." He laced his fingers through hers, the warmth of her skin dispelling the memories of those often dark nights spent tending bar in that freaky old lobby. "He owned the gallery. We talked a lot, and I helped put together a few events, hung a few paintings, did some publicity, that kind of stuff. In return, he agreed to show some of my work. It sold pretty well, so he asked for more, and soon I was painting full time."

His tale was interrupted by the arrival of the first round of food, a colorful array of local dishes and fragrant concoctions. He smiled to the waiter as the man arranged the dishes before them and then continued when they were alone again. "When Christof, the artist, decided he wanted to go back to Europe, he sold me the shop." He clearly remembered the day he received the keys. It was one of the best days of his life, the day he found what he'd been looking for. "And that is how I came to be a gallery owner."

"That is a very New Orleans type of story," she said with a smile. "Do you run it all by yourself?"

"No," he said. "Another painter—an adjunct professor at UNO—comes in and helps me a few days a week. I need the time off to work on my own stuff."

She nodded once and looked away. "Is she pretty?"

"Are you jealous, Prom Dress?" He touched her chin, lifting her eyes back to his. "You needn't be. Joel isn't pretty at all. He's got too much chest hair."

She scoffed, but he saw the flush on her cheeks. "I'm not jealous. I just remember how it used to be."

"Those were good times, but we are older now."

She smiled and lifted her glass. "If not exactly more mature."

Ten laughed. "I'll drink to that," he said and touched his glass to hers.

They each sampled a few bites of the food, making quiet murmurs of appreciation for the culinary delights. New Orleans cuisine was heavy on sauce and butter, cream and rice, spicy concoctions of shrimp and meat. It was heavier than he usually ate, but so tasty.

He took another bite of pecan-crusted alligator sausage and placed his fork aside, needing a break. "How was the first day of your conference? Did you make lots of friends?"

"I did." She dabbed the corners of her mouth with her napkin, then placed it back down on her lap. "I even have a breakfast date for tomorrow."

He raised a single eyebrow. "Hmm, maybe it's my turn to be jealous."

She chuckled and he knew immediately that she was about to yank his chain. "You should be. The very married managing partner of an international digital marketing company wants to talk with me and about ten others about new social media venues. It promises to be a thrilling event." She plucked a fried oyster off one of the plates and popped it in her mouth. Watching her chew was truly a divine experience. "I saw Peter and Melanie today." She leaned toward him, a mischievous grin on her glossy lips. "I think they slept together."

He couldn't care less, but he was amused by her amusement. "What makes you think that?"

She looked around and then moved closer to him, giving her words an air of confidentiality. "They couldn't look each other in the eye any time they were in the same room together. Squirreliness like that could only mean they hooked up."

He moved his chair, closing the small gap between them. "How did you come to that conclusion? We've slept together and we can look each other in the eye."

She met his gaze, only reinforcing his point. "Yeah, but we don't regret it."

That was certainly nice to hear. "You think they regret it?"

"It would make sense if they did. This is a professional conference. They hooked up like a couple of horny teenagers. If people found out, no one would take them seriously. We're supposed to be here to work, not have wild, monkey sex. Their reputations would definitely suffer. Sex and professionalism don't mix."

The waiter came, took their empty plates away, delivered new ones, poured more wine in their glasses, then left. Ten waited for the man to go and then turned back to her. "Do you think they had wild, monkey sex?"

"Actually, no. I think they had really bad sex."

That was his impression as well. "How bad do you think it was?"

She scrunched up her nose. "I bet he's a wet, sloppy kisser."

He grimaced. Sloppy kisses were awful. But there were worse things. "And she probably just laid there too. Didn't move at all."

Stacy nodded, the mischievous glint back in her eyes. "Yup, while he jackhammered away."

Ten recoiled, wincing inwardly. Terrible. "Without making any noise."

She smiled and paused. Tension hung in the silence. "Do you like noise?"

You know that I do. "I like to know that I'm having an effect." He held her gaze. "And I like being affected."

Her eyes gleamed in the dim light and he wondered if she was thinking about the noises she had made with him, the noise they'd made together. He certainly was. "I wonder if he licked her belly button." She looked directly into his eyes. "That especially sucks."

He blinked, appalled and yet completely enamored with her. She was thinking about it. That was one of his best moves. He leaned closer to her, her scent filling his head. "You loved it."

Her gaze dropped to his mouth and his internal thermostat rocketed into the red zone. "Maybe I did."

She was so close; he could almost taste her breath. High-powered tension coiled every muscle in his body. All he had to do was dip his head a half an inch and his lips would be on hers.

The waiter appeared at his elbow and Ten scowled at the man, furious with the interruption. "Yes?" he asked through clenched teeth.

"Would you care for dessert?"

He looked to Stacy, and she shook her head. "No, thank you."

The waiter nodded once, left the check on the table, and walked away. Ten let out a long breath, trying to quell some of the heat racing through his veins. He needed to take it down a notch. This was a night with an old friend, not the start of anything meaningful—especially since that friend would be leaving in a few days. Nothing would come of this. "Should we go see the gallery now?"

She tossed her napkin on the table and rose to her feet. "Yes, I'd like that."

They exited the restaurant and Stacy blew out a long breath. Her heart was racing in her chest, a strong, demanding flutter. She was trying to be good, trying not to let her hormones get out of control, but she didn't think she could stand another close call like that and still keep her sanity intact. If he got that close to her again, she was going to have to go for it and take the kiss she desperately wanted—no matter how heartbreaking the consequences may be.

Ten laced his fingers through hers and led her across the street. Young couples stood outside the bars, smoking and laughing, enjoying the warm night air. She smiled over at him, drunk on wine, on rich food, on the scent of his cologne. It was the perfect New Orleans night and there was magic in the air.

He unlocked the front door and they entered the little blue house. It smelled like potpourri and fresh paint. He flicked on the lights, and a smile curved her lips as she took in the open gallery space. Paintings hung on all four of the walls and several statues were positioned throughout the space. A dark wood table ran along the back of the room, and the cash register sat on top, next to a display of handmade jewelry.

"Here," he said, taking her by the elbow to guide her across the room. "I just finished this one."

They stopped before a large painting done in heavy oils, depicting a Mardi Gras float. The image was dark, bleary, a hazy rendition of night. The crowd was done in silhouette, their backs to the viewer. Bright splashes of color burst through the darkness, sparkling beads thrown to the watchers. Shadow hands reached into the charcoal sky. She could practically hear the music blasting from the float, the people screaming for trinkets. The riders' masks were lewd and comical, exaggerated beastly creatures. Down in the far right corner, there was a single figure in red, a grinning fiend in a scarlet and black mask. He was looking over his shoulder directly at the viewer, his grin impish and sinister, a Mardi Gras devil out for a good time. The card beside it read, *King of Carnival.*

She gaped at the painting, blown away by his talent. She'd no idea he was this good. "This is spectacular, Ten."

In a million years, she would've never thought of Ten capable of being bashful and yet that was the exact look on his face when he simply replied, "Thank you."

She turned from the painting to stroll around the gallery. The art was all very New Orleans centric, images of the city and people, but there were some stylistic differences that didn't quite match up with what she had seen in the Mardi Gras piece. She spun on her heel to face him. "You didn't do all of these, did you?"

"No," he said. He pointed to a painting of a cemetery hanging on the wall near the entrance. "Some of them are Joel's—the professor's—other stuff is from a variety of local artists." He touched the counter, lightly tapping the wood. "I got a really good break when the last owner invited me to show here. I'm just trying to keep the karma going."

Yep, that sounded like Ten. She toured the room again, easily able to pick out his pieces with their bold style, thick paint, and strong, primary colors. And though the images were as straightforward as the man himself, all of his work had a dreamy quality, like looking into a dark and foggy night.

"How's your website look?" she asked, her mind racing with possibilities. She could promote the hell out of his stuff. With what she was certain could only be a few minor tweaks to his publicity plan, he could easily be making three times what he was making now.

He leaned back against the counter, watching her closely. "I have a pretty basic set up."

"Oh, no." She spun around, taking in a full three hundred and sixty degree view of the place. "You need something more than a basic setup. You need something that's going to attract an international client base. Selling to tourists off the street is nice and all, but you could do so much more." Oh, yeah, she was going to make him famous. "We're totally going to build you something from scratch, Ten. Sharpe Designs is going to create a whole new platform for you."

He laughed. "Whoa, Stacy, I don't need all that."

She was so profoundly shocked by his statement, she froze in place. "What do you mean you don't need all that?"

He folded his arms across his chest. "I mean exactly what I said. I don't need a new website."

She blinked, unable to comprehend what he was saying. "Why wouldn't you want to increase your business? You're obviously not doing it for free now. Why not make as much money as you can?"

He shook his head. "I do it because I love it, and I'm lucky enough to make some money from it. But I don't want to spend my time worrying about shipping and rotating stock and constantly updating the site and thinking about traffic and ways to increase my numbers. That all goes with along with this package you want to build for me, doesn't it?"

"We'd do a lot of that for you, but yeah, the material would have to come from you. Don't you want a wider audience?"

"I don't need it. I want to spend my time painting, not advertising. The gallery does fine as it is."

Stacy ground her teeth, forcing herself to back off. What he did with his business was none of her concern. He didn't want her help. He made that clear. Pushing him was only going to make him angry. She should have known what his response was going to be anyway. Ten always did just enough to get by and not a single thing more. He was a 'have a cocktail and let it ride' kind of guy, not an aggressive businessman. "Okay. But if you change your mind…" She dug around in her purse and pulled out her card. "Will you think about it?"

He took the card and tucked it into his wallet. "I will let you know." He pushed himself off the counter and held out his hand to her. "Come on, I should get you back to the Quarter."

She took his hand as the peace offering that it was. Ten was Ten. Success had never meant anything to him. He simply enjoyed what came. "Do I have a curfew?" she asked, teasing him.

"I don't want you to be tired for your meetings tomorrow." He gave her that charming smile that never failed to melt her bones. "I wouldn't want to be a bad influence."

She couldn't help but laugh. He was always a bad influence. Her very own bad influence. And that was why she liked him so much. He allowed her to be free, wild, in a way she never could be in her 'real' life. She put her hand on his chest, the firm muscle warm and solid beneath her palm. "But you haven't shown me everything yet." She nodded toward the ceiling. "What's upstairs?"

He smiled and tension crackled between them, white-hot and electric. "My studio."

"Your studio, huh?" she asked, slowly tracing the outline of his pec. Flirting was never easy for her, but it came so easily with him—as natural and effortless as breathing. "Anything else?"

His gaze flicked to her lips. "My bed."

The look in his eyes made her tingle from her scalp down to her toes. She moved a little closer to him, and he wrapped his arms around her, drawing her into his embrace. "Is it the same one you had when you lived uptown?"

He shook his head slowly and longing uncurled in her belly.

"No, it's new."

She lifted her chin to feel his breath on her lips. "Hey, Ten?"

"Yeah, Stacy?"

"Are you going to kiss me?"

A flash of a grin. "Do you want me to kiss you?"

Her heart pounded, her blood ablaze. "Yes, I do."

He brushed his lips over hers and her legs trembled. She wondered for an insane second if she was going to swoon, but the press of his lips against hers swept all thoughts away. She opened for him, letting him in, letting his taste flood her senses. The whole world vanished and there was only Ten, his lips, his heat, his kiss. She wound her fingers in his dark hair and kissed him harder, savoring all that she had missed.

His fingers twined in her hair and he cupped the back of her head. Hunger exploded in her veins as he took the kiss deeper, making her toes curl in her sandals. On a scale of one to ten, this kiss rated a bazillion. Her arms tightened around him, her body melded to his. They parted with a ravenous gasp and dove in again as church bells rang in the distance, chiming the midnight hour. Stacy poured every bit of emotion, desire, and lust worthy craving into every touch of their lips. The midnight kiss she had been searching for since New Year's Eve had finally come. This was the dream kiss of her life and she was going to savor every bit of it.

The last gong faded into the night, and they parted, breathless, panting. She curled her fingers into the soft hair at the nape of his neck and held on tight. His heart beat against her breast, strong, steady, comforting.

She was grinning like a lunatic when he pulled back, and he looked at her curiously, smoothing the hair off her face. "What?"

She shook her head. It was too ridiculous to even mention and far too crazy to explain. She was not usually a sentimental person and she didn't need him thinking she was a lunatic—well, any more than he already did. And those midnight bells meant it was far later than she thought. She did have a full day ahead of her and there was a long list of things she intended to accomplish. That wouldn't happen if she spent her time sleeping. She placed her hand on his chest and put some distance between them. "You were right. We should get back."

With a single nod, he accepted her wishes, and they gathered their things. He gave her his jacket to wear for the ride back. The night was a little too warm for it, and it was huge on her, but she snuggled into it anyway, enveloped in the scent of his cologne. She gripped him from behind, her arms around his narrow waist, the heat of his body between her thighs. They rode slowly back to the Quarter, and at every stop sign and traffic light, he ran his hands down her bare legs, checking to make sure she was all right and soothing any small hurts. She didn't regret a single pebble, not even the one that bounced off her shin. The pain was totally worth it.

He gave the bike to the valet and escorted up to her room. "Will I see you tomorrow?" he asked as they stopped in front of her door.

She winced. It hurt to have to turn him down, but work had to come first. "I can't. Tomorrow night is an awards dinner I have to attend." A brilliant idea occurred to her and she instantly brightened. Maybe she didn't have to go alone. A lot of the attendees brought their spouses. Surely, she could bring a guest. "Maybe you could be my date?"

He raised a single eyebrow. "Do I need to wear a suit?"

She'd never had the pleasure of seeing him in a suit and the thought made her incredibly happy. She nodded enthusiastically. "Yes."

His laugher tickled her insides. "What time should I be here?"

She bit her lower lip. "It starts at seven. But we can be late if you can't get here on time because of the gallery."

"No, that's fine," he said and tucked a lock of her hair behind her ear. The soft caress of his fingertips heated her skin, made her want to giggle and swoon. The littlest things he did just about killed her. "Joel will be in tomorrow. It's one of my studio days. He opens and closes up by himself. I can get here anytime."

"Great." She slipped out of his jacket and handed it back to him. "Thanks for dinner, Ten. I had a really good time."

He shrugged the jacket on. "So did I."

She smiled at him, wanting him to kiss her again. She moved a little closer to hopefully encourage that action. "I guess I'll see you tomorrow then."

He nodded, and when he dipped his head, everything part of her shivered with excitement. She lifted her chin, ready to taste him again, when the elevator doors slid open, vomiting out a riotous group of convention attendees. One of the women screamed laughter as they moved down the hall to their various rooms.

Stacy dropped her arms from around him and immediately missed the warmth of his body. This was not cool. What was she thinking? They shouldn't be making out in front of her room. It was totally unprofessional.

Ten nodded and touched her cheek, a light caress of his thumb that heated her all the way down to her toes. "Goodnight, Stacy."

"Goodnight, Ten." She smiled a little sadly as she watched him walk down the hallway and then disappear into the elevator.

Chapter Three

Stacy entered the overly air-conditioned meeting room and took an empty seat near the back. People arrived in singles and in pairs for the *Global Trends and Customer Behavior* presentation, filing into the room in a bevy of noise and fresh-brewed coffee. She spotted Peter and Melanie sitting on opposite sides, studiously not looking at one another. It seemed Melanie had found another companion; she was talking closely with an older man in a very nice suit. Peter was alone.

Stacy shook her head and looked away. She felt bad for him, but she was so glad Peter had fallen for the other woman. Where would she be now if he had not? They probably would have never gone to Bourbon Street, which meant that she would not have seen Ten. She guessed she owned them a debt in a way.

The first speaker, a vice president of something that she didn't quite catch, tapped the microphone on the podium to make sure it was working. The feedback made the crowd wince and earned him jeers from his colleagues on the stage. Cold air blasted through the many vents, and Stacy folded her arms under her breasts and shivered. Most of the rooms in the hotel had been freezing; a thing she hadn't anticipated when she'd packed, but should have. She hoped the dinner tonight was not going to be this cold. The dress she brought for the event was thin and not going to keep her warm.

She hugged herself tighter as another blast of frigid air assaulted her. She could really use Ten's jacket right about now. She should have kept it. Thoughts of last night, of him, warmed her from the inside out. She couldn't believe how much she wanted to see him again. He'd crossed her mind many times over the years, one of the great "what ifs" of her life. She'd never seriously thought she'd see him again, and if she had, she'd always imagined that it would be friendly enough, but nothing serious. But five years had changed a lot. Changed him. He had a gallery now, a business, something he loved. He was not the same frivolous young man he had been.

She smiled, lost in the memories of those terribly wonderful days. She'd spent most of her time at the restaurant, serving jambalaya and gumbo to tourists from all over the world. Some people were nice, but for the most part, it had been hard, thankless work and the customers could be atrocious. The Cabin paid her a whopping two dollars and thirteen cents an hour, and instead of tips she'd been given prayer cards some nights, Mardi Gras beads on others, and always, every night, received some sort of lewd, crude, offer that made her stomach churn. But the staff had been awesome, some of the best people she'd ever worked with, and even at the worst moments, she was comforted by the fact that it wasn't going to be her life forever. When she wasn't at work, she was attending job fairs, refining her résumé, and partying hard. She'd had a blast and loved every minute of it, but only suffered the slightest regret when she'd decided to take one of the jobs offers she received and leave New Orleans behind.

Ten and his two roommates—all of whom worked at the Cabin—hosted her going away party. And they knew how to throw a proper bash. There were seven different kinds of Jell-O shots and kegs of beer and bottles of vodka, rum, and bourbon. There were mixed drinks, blended drinks, shots and mind erasers and martinis. People got messy drunk in that old house by Tulane University. Unfortunately, she had to keep herself mostly under control. She had an early flight in the morning and she did not want to face the airport hungover. So, she kept it to a minimum and drank lightly, mingling with her coworkers, saying goodbye to everyone, moving from room to room. She'd probably been at the party for a good hour before she ran into Ten.

He was coming down the ancient, creaking wooden staircase a beer in his hand and grin on his lips. Her heart still fluttered remembering how handsome he was, how much she had wanted him.

She didn't even know precisely how it had happened, the details lost to time and alcohol. One minute they were on the couch, then next he was tugging on her hand, and she was following him upstairs. His room was on the top floor, under the slanting eaves. It was dim, lit only by the street lamps through the open windows. The heavy scent of night-blooming jasmine hung in the thick air. They sat down on his bed, a full-size model outfitted in navy sheets, a musty old thing only a guy could ever sleep on comfortably. She'd giggled like a madman, all geeked out about being alone with him.

And when he kissed her for the first time, it was like something out of her wildest dreams. A kiss so good, she felt it in every cell in her body. It left her breathless, trembling, longing for more. If that kiss had been any different, any less intense or sincere, she probably would not have slept with him that night. Maybe she would have fooled around with him a bit, but nothing more than that. But that kiss changed everything. They made love all night, taking little breaks to rest and cuddle, and then the morning came and with it, her departure for the life she had mapped out for herself ever since she was ten years old.

And though she sought it, pursed it, did everything in her power to replicate it, she never felt anything remotely like that first kiss she shared with him again.

Until last night.

The audience applauded and Stacy blinked. She let out a long breath to calm her racing heart. The memory was so vivid, the emotion so raw, she had to shake herself back into the present. Another speaker approached the podium, and she forced herself to focus. She was not here to reminisce about the past.

"Hello, everyone," the speaker said, and Stacy recognized him from his many profile pictures. Martin Padgett, president of MarketBlitz, Inc., and one of the most respected authorities on targeted marketing in the entire industry. He smiled at the audience, and she sat up straighter, curious about his presentation. "I'm so glad we have this room today. The artic chill in here will keep you all alert no matter how boring I get."

The audience chuckled, and Padgett gave them a charming grin. He was a handsome man, probably in his early fifties, with thick salt and pepper hair and a wide smile. There was a confidence about him that was very appealing. He was a man who knew he had no trouble holding the attention of a room. He reminded her a lot of Ten. They shared the same strong poise.

"I'm here today to talk to you about bringing some hedonism to marketing. We're in the perfect setting for it, aren't we?" He paused as people murmured their agreement. "As technology advances, it becomes easier for us to live lazy, sedentary, solitary lives. But the cultural shifts we're seeing in the market are showing a move toward a more interactive, intense experience. People want to be engaged. They want passion. Full-frontal immersion." He smiled. "Kind of like Bourbon Street on Friday night."

The audience grinned back. He really did have charisma.

"We love our plans and charts and outlooks, predictions and forecasts and research studies. Those things are fine, great, useful tools. I'm not telling you to dump all that. But in this taciturn and ever more serious world, to really appeal to the people out there, you must incorporate an aspect of silliness, an outright frivolity in your approach. It gives the human touch that is sadly lacking in so many things. I want you all to be hedonistic in your approach. Take a chance and do one thing so outside the box most people tell you it's a waste of your time and will never work. Just one time per project, go out of your comfort zone and do something outlandish, a pure and total risk."

Stacy was a bit uncomfortable with his advice. She liked her charts and plans, but she saw the wisdom. Sharpe Designs tended to rely heavily on social media outlets, but there were plenty of other venues she could explore that fell outside the norm. She made some quick notes in her tablet about the first few things that came to mind. New York offered a wealth of opportunities. There was always someone out there trying something new, developing some new program, some bigger, better, faster, sexier way to share information. She would consult with her staff when she got back and brainstorm an extensive list of options.

"There is no such thing as an absolute single best marketing strategy. Not anymore." Padgett met the eyes of the audience over the lectern. "Thinking that way is only going to hold you back. And make no mistake—you will be left behind."

***

Morning sunlight streamed through the windows of Ten's studio, golden highlights illumining the painting he had set up on the easel. Joel's voice drifted up from the gallery below, the murmur of indistinct conversation. It sounded like business was good down there, and he smiled, imagining the professor doing his thing, selling art and charming the ladies.

He returned his attention to the painting before him, tapping his fingers lightly against his thigh as he gave it a critical eye. It had been almost a year since he'd last worked on this piece, and though he'd put her aside, she was never forgotten. The image was burned into his mind's eye, into his heart. When he started her, he'd known even then that he'd never be able to capture the truth of moment and yet he did it anyway, helpless not to. And now she was his great, unfinished masterpiece—the one piece he couldn't quite get right, but could never abandon.

He took a sip of coffee, looked to his brushes and then away. He probably should dust or something in here. Maybe do that bookshelf project he'd been thinking about for months. And there was never a bad time to do the gallery's books. His gaze flicked back to the painting and he clenched it his jaw. If he was going to work on it, then he needed to get to work. Stalling did not accomplish anything. But, he wasn't sure how to begin. Or if he even should begin. Did he really want to resurrect this old ghost?

His eyes touched on small details, on the hints of red and pink and white. The portrait was much lighter and brighter than his usual work, depicting a beautiful woman, nude and wrapped in a sheet, sitting on a bed, looking back over her shoulder. He'd tried to capture that morning perfectly, how the pale dawn light filtered through the white curtains of his bedroom windows in that ramshackle old house he used to live in near Tulane. Her skin, pale and creamy, her cheeks pink from their lovemaking, the slight flush that had taken him months to blend properly. He ran his finger over the curve of her hip, the layers of paint it took to replicate her porcelain skin. Her red hair in the painting was bright and coppery, but he saw now that he had it all wrong. Her hair was more like fire than copper.

The hair he could fix, but it was the look on her face that gave him trouble, the curve of her lips was never quite right. When he told her how much he had always wanted her, her lips had been caught in something between a smile and gasp, parted, but only slightly, wet from his kiss. That look was what he could never capture, what made the painting wrong and incomplete. But maybe the memory was too mixed up with his own longing to ever be right. He could see the brushstrokes where he'd tried to alter her face to reflect more of what he'd wanted, rather then what actually occurred. Because no matter how much he thought he saw her love for him in her eyes, in her smile, on her lips, she had left—with no intention of ever retuning. She did want him, he'd seen that clearly, but she'd also wanted to leave and that was what he was always trying to ignore when he worked on her. It was the thing he needed to address if he ever wanted to get it right.

He took another sip of coffee and stared out of the window, lost in the past. The year he'd spent at the Cabin with her had been one of the best years of his life. Even going to the bar after a shift was an adventure, full of laughter and flirtation. She always made him feel so special, like everything he said mattered, and she was smart, so he always had to up his game just to keep up with her. And every time he was rewarded with her smile, he practically glowed inside.

He touched the painting's lips, recalling the taste of her mouth. Kissing her again was as good as it had been the very first time— maybe even better. He licked his lips, igniting the memory, recalling the texture of tongue, her soft sigh against his lips. Everything in him stirred, and he closed his eyes, letting the longing, the desire, flow over him. Unguarded, unchecked, he blocked out all the reasons it was wrong and let himself feel the pure emotion of all that he felt for her.

His gaze returned to the canvas, and he reached for a brush out of the old coffee can he had welded to the easel. He mixed a new shade of red on his palette, lightly threading the color through the tumultuous waves of her hair. It had been longer then, flowing down to the center of her back, a cascade of waves, tangled and curled from their love. Strands stuck to the side of her face, to her long throat, her shoulder. Wisps faded out into drops of white fire in the early morning sunlight.

He sat back and looked over his work. He still had a lot left to do. He'd managed to capture the correct brown for her eyes, not chocolate or caramel or whiskey, but a swirl of all of them blended and individual. But he'd left out the flecks of gold and verdant green. And her lips were nowhere near right. They were too plump, too garish, screaming sex when sex had really been only a small part of what that morning meant. He was going to have to completely redo them. He focused on her hair for now though, the least impossible part of the whole doomed enterprise.

What if she had stayed? he wondered as he touched up a fiery wave. What if she'd forsaken everything for him and stayed, granting his heart's fondest wish. Would she still even be his? Five years was a long time. Would they have really gotten together and made it work? Would they be married now, thinking about children, thinking about mortgages and taxes and in-laws? Or would they have just faded into a broken dream? A failed relationship, leaving them both sullen and heartbroken? So many possibilities, so many outcomes.

He added a hit of gold to a strand of hair framing her face. He worked hard, blending and reshaping, trying to merge the truth of the present with his memories of the past. Things had changed.

But that was the problem, wasn't it? Things had changed and they had lives a thousand miles apart. Real, adult lives. And the bottom line was, she was not going to stay in New Orleans, and he did not want to go to New York. Not that she'd asked him of course. And she probably wouldn't. She had no reason to. Sure, they got along, but they barely knew one another anymore. They shared a lot of great memories, but those things were long in the past.

But the minute he saw her, he thought about it. Could he go to New York?

He put the brush aside with a sigh. He was getting ahead of himself. He was going to see her for dinner tonight, not to propose. Running away to New York was a nice thought, but he had to be real. Think beyond the fantasy of making love to her every day. So, he goes to New York. What then? Would he move in with her? Where would he paint? He'd need studio space. A place of his own to be alone and create. He certainly couldn't do it in the middle of her living room. If she even had a living room. New York apartments weren't famous for their size. Or their low, low prices. Which begged the question, how would he make money? To move, he'd have to close the shop. New York wasn't cheap and not exactly a great place to be an artist. His work sold well here, but would it there? How would he even show his stuff? He'd have no connections, no foundation. He didn't want to go back to restaurant work. Just the thought made him cringe. And so, he'd have no job and no connections. He'd be totally dependent upon her for everything. There was no way he could live like that. Besides, he had a life here, one he liked. A business. This was what he wanted to do with his life. He didn't want to give it up.

The front door of the shop slammed shut and Ten blinked, his reverie shattered. How long had he been staring off into space, dreaming up nonsense? Too long, judging from the light coming in through the studio windows. It was decidedly darker than it had been when last he looked. The day was practically gone. He looked down at the paint on his hands, his clothes. He needed to get ready now if he was going to be on time for dinner. He sighed. It was not like him to waste his time thinking about pointless things. He was a one day at a time kind of guy. All this planning and scheming—that was Stacy's thing, not his.

His gaze shifted back to the painting. Better, but still not right. He tapped his finger against his own lips as he contemplated hers. What was missing? He picked up a brush and added a hit of gloss to her lips. He smiled to himself. Would her lips be so welcoming tonight? So warm and lush and filled with promise? He hoped so.

He jumped off the stool and stripped off his clothes, tossing them into the separate pile where he put all his painting attire. He slid the closet's French doors open and peered inside. He owned two suits, one light gray, one charcoal. After a moment's hesitation, he chose darker one, the custom-tailored suit he'd had made when he won a Community Arts Award last year. It'd cost him a month's salary, but it was worth every penny. He looked good in it. He thought that she would agree.

He laid the suit out on his bed and his gaze drifted toward the nightstand, the drawer where he kept his condoms. Just the thought triggered a flash of heat in his groin. Maybe it wasn't a good idea to bring any along. Should he tempt fate? All they'd shared so far was a single kiss. A great kiss, but still, just a kiss. He didn't want to force the issue, and he had no expectations. The fact that they'd slept together in past meant nothing and had no bearing on the present. He knew that.

Still, he thought of the way she had kissed him last night, her fingers in his hair, the press of her body against his. What would have happened if those people had not come out of the elevator? Maybe nothing, but then again, maybe something.

He crossed the room and opened the drawer. No expectations, he told himself as he slid a condom into his wallet. This was just in case. The memory of her scent, her taste, filled his thoughts, and he added one more. Just in case, he reminded himself, and went off to the shower with a big smile on his face.

Chapter Four

Her lipstick was not right. Stacy leaned closer to the bathroom mirror, her nose almost touching the glass. She needed to get her lips just right. She wanted them to be so appealing, Ten would not resist any urge he might have to kiss them. She was not going to miss out on another opportunity with him tonight.

A knock on her door caught her attention and her stomach fluttered. He was here. She gave the neck of her black Donna Karan dress a quick tug to show off a bit more cleavage, then opened the door. The man waiting for her on the threshold was breathtaking, dapper and handsome in a dark suit, with a vibrant green tie and shined shoes. Her heart beat a little faster, her blood became a little hot.

"Hi," she said, grabbing her clutch purse off the dresser. Her voice was more breathless than she wanted to be, and she hoped her school girl excitement didn't show too much on her face.

"Hi." His gaze touched on her hair, her face, the bare expanse of her skin, every flick of his gaze making her tingle inside. "You look sensational."

When he took her arm and escorted her downstairs, she felt like Cinderella at the ball. There was a dashing man by her side and the night was full of promise. She felt beautiful with him, confident in every way, and she noticed that heads turned when they entered the room. She was the luckiest woman in the world.

The ballroom was filled with a sea of round tables, adorned in shell-pink linens, gleaming silverware, and crystal glassware. They choose seats on the far left side of the room, close enough to see the stage, but far enough away that they could sneak out if they wanted to. Not that she wanted to sneak out, she told herself as he held out a chair for her. Just an option. Just in case.

He sat down beside her, and she caught a dash of crimson in his otherwise dark hair. She reached over and touched the soft strands, crumbling the dry red substance between her fingers. "You have paint in your hair."

He grinned sheepishly. "Yeah, that happens sometimes."

"Are you working on something new?" she asked, brushing the last remnants away.

"No, it's actually something I've been working on for a while now."

"Did you finish it?"

He shook his head, reached out, and hooked a stray lock of hair behind her ear. "Not yet."

She knew Ten well enough to know that he was holding something back, but she couldn't imagine what it could be. "I'd love to see it."

He nodded once and she waited for him to tell her more, but Peter Walker sat down next to them, destroying the moment. She and Ten greeted Peter and his companion, a VP at a firm she was not familiar with.

Tuxedoed waiters circulated the room with pitchers of water and bottles of champagne and the ballroom hummed with greetings and small talk. Stacy sipped her champagne. Ten's knee touched hers beneath the table, the warm press of his leg as delightful as the bubbles in the champagne. And just as heady.

The servers brought around trays of covered entrees and presented them to the guests. She lifted the lid on her plate and cringed when she recognized the saucy rice dish. Crawfish étouffée.

She poked the tiny shellfish with her fork. "You know, I've never really been able to eat these things ever since you took me to that boil."

He laughed. "You gotta suck da heads, sweetheart."

She let out an exaggerated shudder. They'd stumbled upon the outdoor festival and crawfish boil while strolling along the Riverwalk one evening. Styrofoam containers of the mudbugs were being sold for just one dollar a pound, all proceeds going to benefit music programs in New Orleans area schools. She was always ready to try new things, especially for a good cause, but that experience had been a little much for her. She grimaced at her plate and pushed another crawfish aside. "All I remember were those terrible"—she shuddered again— "insectile legs. They were everywhere." She stuck out her tongue. "Those beady, little eyes, the antennae…"

Ten reached over with his fork and speared a crawfish on her plate. He held it up. "It's safe now. Totally leg free. Give it a try."

She gave him a dubious look, but he did not drop the fork. She had two choices, either accept the challenge or forever deal with him calling her a wimp. Since she couldn't allow that, she put her hand on his wrist. His pulse was strong beneath her fingertips. She gave him a big smile, dipped her head, and took the fork into her mouth. The spicy sauce exploded on her tongue, a sharp, hot taste that burned nicely. She chewed the crawfish slowly, his gaze fixed on her mouth, hunger burning in his eyes. Just for his benefit, she licked her lips when she was done. "Yum."

He reached over and touched the corner of her mouth, a gentle caress of his thumb that lined the edge of her bottom lip. He held up his hand so she could see the drop of sauce and everything in her went liquid when he slowly, deliberately licked it off his finger. "Yum indeed."

Stacy thanked every single god she could think of that the lights dimmed at that moment, saving her from exploding. Her legs were trembling under the table, her breath short. A round of applause broke out when the emcee took the stage and she swallowed a huge gulp of champagne to steady herself. She needed to maintain some kind of decorum. The last thing she wanted to do was embarrass herself by attacking him in public. That was no way to make an impression.

The awards ceremony commenced with the usual fanfare and speeches. Stacy picked up her champagne glass, but quickly put it aside. She needed to be productive tonight. The conference was winding down and she still hadn't secured a panel spot for next year. She decided her goal for the evening was to meet five new people. It didn't matter who they were or where they were from, just five new people to connect with. She scanned the crowd, trying to decide who looked the most interesting.

Ten leaned over, his thigh touching hers as he moved in close to her side. "One day you're going to be up there."

She smiled at the thought, the desire for it swelling in her chest. "That would be nice." She put her napkin aside, finished with the heavy dinner. "Ultimately, I'd like to sponsor an award though."

He laughed softly. "Can you ever be happy with less than the absolute best?"

"No," she said, her eyebrows furrowed. "Why should I?"

"Because sometimes it's nice to be in the moment you're in, and not always thinking about the next, better thing."

She frowned. "I just know that I can always do better."

He held up his palms to her. "Don't get me wrong. I admire your drive. I always have. But I wonder if you ever take the time to live in the present."

"I'm living in the present right now."

"Are you?" he asked, amused. "Or are you thinking about who you want to talk to once these speeches are over?"

Her cheeks flushed. She hadn't realized she was so transparent. "This is for my work."

"I know," he said. "And it's going do great things for your career." He held up his glass, admiring the liquid within. "But when you drink champagne, you should taste the champagne. Let it linger your tongue. Feel the bubbles in your head, your nose, your throat. Let it tickle your senses." He held out the glass to her. "Don't miss the full experience because you're wondering if there's another, better bottle somewhere on the other side of the room."

She picked up her drink and touched it to his. The glasses made a soft clank when they met. The fizz tickled her nose when she brought the glass to her lips, the bubbles exploding when they touched her tongue. She tasted fruit and wood, crisp and refreshing, and she was surprised by how delicate and effervescent it was. She had never noticed before.

He watched her closely, a small smile playing on his generous lips. "Nice?"

"Very," she said and put the glass aside. "But stopping to smell the champagne isn't going to get me where I want to be in life. Don't you want more than you have now? I do."

He shook his head. "I'm happy with what I have now."

"How is the even possible, Ten? Isn't getting ahead the meaning of life? The American Dream?"

He leaned over and brushed a strand of hair off her shoulder. "It's not my dream."

"But you must want it in some way," she insisted. "If you didn't, you'd still be waiting tables on Bourbon Street."

"No, that's a totally different thing. I stopped doing that because it didn't please me anymore. I wanted to find something new. Something I liked. Something I could do forever."

Her eyes narrowed. "And what happens if you find yourself unsatisfied again one day?"

He shrugged. "Then, on that day, I'll find something else. But I don't think that's going to happen. I've found my thing. I love what I do."

A loud round of applause cut off any further conversation and the lights went up, signaling the end of the ceremony. People began rising from their seats. One of the men she'd pinpointed earlier left the ballroom with a glamorous woman on his arm. In fact, most people were leaving in pairs. Everywhere she looked, people were coupling up, heading off in different directions. Maybe tonight was not the night for networking. She looked to Ten, studying his profile in the low light. Maybe tonight she should take his advice and enjoy the moment. "How would you feel about having a night cap with me?"

He smiled, but she could tell from his raised eyebrow that he was surprised. "I'd feel pretty good about that. Do you have someplace in mind?"

"Well," she said, the heat rising to her cheeks from pure anticipation alone. This was a good idea. "My room has an extensive array of liquors in the minibar." She leaned closer to him, dropping her voice down low. "It even has chips."

"Chips?" he asked, the gleam in his eyes turning mischievous. "Chips are pretty good."

She nodded, trying to maintain a serious face. "Three. Different. Kinds."

He held her gaze. "That sounds positively decadent."

She didn't think she'd ever liked anybody nearly as much as she liked Ten. Being with him was always the best kind of adventure—fun and flirty and a little bit dangerous. Tonight was going to be a good night to spend some long overdue quality time with him. This might be their last chance. She smiled at him, but then frowned when a tap came upon her shoulder.

"Stacy," Peter said and tapped her again. She scrunched up her nose, making a face at Ten, and then grudgingly turned to Peter.

"Yes?" she asked, not bothering to hide her annoyance.

Peter was completely oblivious to her ire. "We just heard there's a small gathering going on upstairs in the presidential suite. Would you care to join us?"

Stacy's eyes widened. A private party? This was not an opportunity she was going to miss. She grabbed Ten's arm. "We'd love to join you."

Peter smiled. "Fantastic. Let's head up."

She turned to Ten and winced. This was probably not how he wanted to spend the night—especially after her promise of tasty chips. "I'm sorry."

He touched her cheek and then offered her his arm. "Honey, you're not here on vacation." She slipped her arm though his and they followed after Peter toward the elevator. "Let's go meet these VIPs."

The presidential suite was on the top floor of the hotel and featured a breathtaking panoramic view of the city. The lavish sitting area was adorned with some of the industry's top figures. She spotted two information gurus, a slew of vice presidents, a lone CEO. The party had an air of happening for some time, and Stacy figured most of these people had skipped the awards dinner, opting for cocktails instead.

She took a deep breath and surveyed the room. Opportunities were everywhere, chances to make valuable connections, learn something new, gain a new opening. The possibilities of what she could garner from this night were endless and expediential.

"One thing at a time," Ten said, close to her ear. "You don't need to take over the entire world tonight."

She smiled and shook her head. She really needed to stop being so transparent. "What makes you think that's what I was thinking?"

"Gee, Brain, I don't know," he said, with a grin. "What do we do every night?"

They crossed the classically furnished living room to the make-shift bar set up on a slightly elevated platform near the entertainment center. They were given two glasses of red wine by the man staffing the station.

"Am I so predictable?" she asked, as they moved aside to let other people approach the bar.

"No, I've just seen that look on your face before. I saw it every time you left work and decided you were going to ace your interview for that day."

She met his gaze. "I've always known what I wanted. And I've worked hard to stand in this room with you. But this is only one of the first steps toward what I really want."

He ran his knuckles over her cheek, a light caress that heated her skin and touched her heart. "I know."

She looked out into the room, at the people in business attire and formal wear gathered in couples and groups, talking quietly, exchanging information, doing business. This was her element and exactly where she wanted to be. She flashed Ten a quick grin and then squared her shoulders. "Are you ready?"

He gestured her forward. "I'll follow your lead."

She spotted an empty space on a couch next to a sharply dressed couple. Ten followed her across the room, and as they got closer, she recognized the man as one of the speakers from the workshop she had attended earlier in the day. She approached them with a smile and pointed to the space. "Are these seats taken?"

The man smiled. "No, please, join us. I'm Martin Padgett, and this is my wife, Linda."

Stacy smiled back. "Thanks. I'm Stacy Saunders, and this is Tennyson Landry." She sat, smoothing her dress down over her thighs. "I really enjoyed your presentation."

Martin beamed. "Thank you. I just hope I didn't bore everyone too much." He took a sip of his wine. "Who do you both work for?"

"I'm with a boutique web design firm called Sharpe Designs in New York, and Ten is an artist here in New Orleans."

"An artist?" Martin asked. "Do you do freelance work for Stacy? We're always looking for great freelance graphic artists."

Ten laughed. "No, I'm much more traditional. Paint on canvas."

Stacy nodded. "You should check out his gallery on Magazine Street if you have time. He's got some great stuff."

"Well, we have been thinking about doing some remodeling," Linda said. "Do you have a card?"

"I do." Ten pulled out his wallet and handed her his card.

"We'll look you up even if we don't make it to the gallery,"

Martian said. "I'm sure Stacy had a hand in your website, so we'll get to see her firm's work while we're at it."

Stacy shifted uncomfortably, but Ten just smiled. "She's still in the process of convincing me to overhaul my site." He put his arm around her shoulders. "I'm just about sold."

"We're always working, aren't we?" Martin said to Stacy with a twinkle in his eye. "I convinced a restaurant owner to let me redo his entire media kit while we were at lunch."

Linda rolled her eyes dramatically. "They're terrible, aren't they, Tennyson? They're lucky we're such patient and under-standing people." She patted her husband's knee affectionately. "Not everyone would sit through a sales pitch during lunch and still find it romantic."

"I think it was more the setting than the company that gave it any romance," Martin said, and everyone laughed.

From the conspiratorial way Linda spoke to Ten, it was obvious she thought they were a couple. Stacy liked the assumption, and was glad Ten didn't seemed inclined to correct her. Linda was right. She was lucky to have Ten. Other guys would have prob-ably ditched her the moment she failed to follow through on the promises she implied during dinner. She was certain this was not what he wanted to do with his night, and yet there he was beside her, being as charming as ever, helping her made her connections and do her job. She put hand on Ten's thigh and gave it a gentle squeeze. "We are very lucky indeed, Linda."

"Speaking of romantic," Linda said. "Since you live here, Tennyson, tell us a good place to have dinner. Somewhere very expensive." She winked at her husband. "I deserve it."

Ten smiled, his hand dropping down from Stacy's shoulders to circle her waist. "Well, we went to Blanchard's last night. It's just a short cab ride from here. It's one of my favorite places."

Stacy nodded. "It was fantastic. The food was incredible. And the courtyard was beautiful."

Martin leaned close. "Do you have their account yet? If not, I might take it."

She grinned at him, pouncing on the opportunity. "It's all yours if I can get a quote in your next article on market trends."

Martin laughed. "I like the way you think, Stacy Saunders. Here's my card, give me yours. Email me when you get home and we'll set something up. I'm actually thinking about addressing branding and social media. Does that sound like something you'd like to talk about?"

"Absolutely." Stacy could have squealed with delight. "It's an important topic at my firm."

He tucked her card into his wallet and then smiled as a man in a very expensive suit walked by. "Oliver!" he called, and the dapper man paused and smiled.

"Oliver, I'd like you to meet Stacy and Tennyson. Stacy works for a boutique web design firm in New York. She's going to be a major source in my next article on branding." He turned to them. "Oliver is the chief technology officer at Engage Digital Media in San Jose."

"A pleasure to meet you both," Oliver said and shook their hands.

"Oliver and I were talking earlier about viable alternatives to Facebook," Martin said. He waved the man toward an empty chair a few paces away. "Join us, please. I think Stacy might be able to offer some valuable insight to that discussion."

She squeezed Ten's leg, and he gave her a one-armed hug. The night was turning out to be better than she expected.

***

It was well after midnight when she and Ten stumbled out of the elevator and onto her floor. She had five business cards stuffed in her purse, three contacts for article quotes, and an invitation to a luncheon when she got back New York. It had been a very productive, though thoroughly exhausting night.

They paused by her door and she rested her fingertips on the handle. "Thank you."

His eyebrows shot up. "For what?"

She put her hand on his shoulder and looked up into his eyes. "For playing the good husband tonight."

He kissed her lightly on the lips, a barely-there peck that sent jolts of electricity rocketing down her spine. "You did an amazing job, Stacy. You earned that promotion."

"Thank you," she said again, touched to her very core. His praise was insanely flattering, warming her inside in a way no amount of business cards ever could. She tapped the metal door handle with her fingernails and asked the question that had been lingering in the back of her mind all night. "Are you still in the mood for chips?"

His grin was pure wickedness. "I do like chips."

Her nerve-endings sizzled as she slid the key card in the lock. The lock disengaged with a loud snap, and she swung the door wide open. Her pulse galloped as Ten followed her inside, and she was a little breathless when she sat down on the bed and kicked off her shoes. He pushed the pillows up against the headboard and sat down beside her. She was very aware of the heat of his body next to hers, the clean, brisk scent of his cologne.

He ran his fingertip down the inside of her forearm, his light caresses raising the fine hair on her body. "Is there a reward for being such a good husband?"

She smiled, her heart beating a little faster. "Are you flirting with me, Tennyson Landry?"

His gaze flicked from her eyes to her lips back to her eyes again. "I just want to know if I earned those chips."

She laughed and poked him in the side. Now that she was finally sitting down and didn't to be one hundred and fifty percent *on*, bone-deep fatigue washed over her. The yawn that came surprised her with its force, so wide it made her jaw crack.

"Did you just yawn?" he asked, laughing.

"I'm sorry," she said and then yawned again. She pressed her fingertips to her lips. "I've been up since five and smiling for hours. I think it's finally catching up with me."

"Here," he said, turning her around so that her back was to him. "Let me see."

He rubbed her shoulders, the back of her neck, the center of her spine. His fingers dug into the tight spots, patiently working out all the kinks. He cupped her shoulder and when his knuckles pressed just under the blade, she melted in his arms.

"Good?" he asked, gently kneading her tired muscles.

"So good."

She floated in the place of blissful relaxation his touch sent her and after a while her head started to feel heavy and her eyes drifted closed. She leaned back against him, and his arms went around her waist. She snuggled deeper into his warmth, burrowing into his embrace. He was very comfortable, and she sighed contently.

He lifted his feet off the floor and settled back on the bed, cradling her against his chest. She purred like a happy cat and stretched out on top of him. He kissed the top of her head, his breath warm on her scalp, and every part of her tingled.

She looked up at him, into his dark green eyes and he slowly traced her cheekbone, a gentle caress that stoked a low burn deep in her core. She nuzzled his palm, the rough callouses on his hand scraping against her cheek. Tension and electricity scorched the air between them, a current of pure, white-hot energy. She lifted her chin, and he dipped his head to meet her parted lips.

Their tongues touched, retreated, touched again. She tasted his hunger, mirroring his desire. He teased her with light kisses and little nips, playful licks and soft sighs before diving into her, taking all that she offered. Kissing him was everything she always dreamed a kiss should be and she wound her fingers into his soft hair, savoring all of him.

They parted for a breath, a break, a chance to caress and explore. She rested her head against his chest while she traced the line of his jaw, his dark stubble tickling her fingertips. His heartbeat was strong beneath her cheek, a soothing, steady rhythm. Fatigue washed over her and her limbs grew heavy. It was so warm in his arms, so safe and secure, she decided to close her eyes for one second.

Chapter Five

Stacy was having the best dream of her life. She was in bed with someone warm and comfortable, someone who smelled good and held her gently. Strong arms circled her waist, holding her tightly against a lean, hard body. She snuggled deeper into her phantom lover, savoring the illusion while it lasted. Soon she would wake up and find herself alone in bed—just like she always was.

Her dream man shifted behind her, drawing her closer. She could vividly imagine the sensation of warm breath on the back of her neck, and the tingly stirrings of arousal settled deep in her belly. Her heart ached for the imaginary feelings that welled in her chest, feelings she often longed for, but pushed aside for more practical goals. She'd always dated with a purpose, always with an eye toward what kind of future she would have with the man with whom she was sharing dinner. She never considered that the simple pleasure of waking up beside someone who cared, being safe in their arms, was all that really mattered.

Soft kisses brushed her cheek, her neck, her shoulder. She shivered as prickles of heat broke out over her skin. She had no idea she had such an active and intense imagination. This was a dream for the record books.

The arms drew tighter around her and she nestled deeper into his warmth. What had she been doing last night that brought on this wonderful delusion? Whatever it was, she wanted to do it again—maybe every night for the rest of her life.

She sighed and then her eyes flew open, the dream shattered by a blaring alarm. She rolled over and slapped the unfamiliar clock. With a pained groan, she sat up, finally cognizant enough to realize that she was not at home. She was in a hotel room in New Orleans.

Fingers traced the curve of her spine and she glanced over her shoulder to find Ten looking up at her with sleep-hooded eyes.

"Hey," he said, and reached up to touch her cheek, a light caress that made her shiver delightfully.

Even wearing last night clothes, he was still incredibly hot. His dark hair was tousled and there was a shadow of stubble on his jaw and everything about him made her insides turn completely liquid.

"You let me sleep," she said, as the night came back to her.

He sat up. "You were tired."

Her heart swelled as she let her gaze roam over him. Her good husband. It would be so easy be in love with him. If only real life could be that dream—because that was the only way they were ever going to be together. She gave his tie a little tug. "I guess I owe you some chips."

He chuckled and rose out of bed, stretched his arms over his head. His shirt and jacket rode up, affording her a slight glimpse of his flat stomach, the trail of dark hair just below his navel. "Will I see you tonight?"

A crystalline memory of kissing her way down his torso years ago flashed through her mind. She had to lick her suddenly dry lips before she could speak again. "This is the last day of the conference, so everything ends kind of early. I should be done by four."

Something flashed in his eyes, there and gone before she could see what it was. "The last day, huh?"

Her heart was heavy, the weight of her impeding departure suddenly very real. "Yeah."

He took a deep breath, then smiled brightly. "Then we'll have to do something special. Text me when you're done, and I'll come get you."

"Okay."

He walked around the bed to her, and she reached up to smooth down his wrinkled lapels. She'd always thought her taste in men ran exclusively toward clean-cut guys in high-powered suits, but unshaven, rumpled Tennyson Landry was maybe the sexiest thing she'd ever had the pleasure to witness.

She stood on her tiptoes to meet his lips for another one of his incredible kisses, but the alarm clock blared again, scaring the crap out of her. She spun around and slapped the blasted thing again, hoping she hit the off button this time, instead of the snooze. She turned back to him with a crooked smile. "I'm sorry."

"It's okay," he said cupping her face in his palm. He ran his thumb over her bottom lip, and then pulled back, letting his hand fall back to his side. "I should get going."

She walked him to the door, and they paused on the threshold. "Let's go to The Asylum tonight. For old time's sake."

The Asylum was a dark, little hole-in-wall bar on Decatur where they often ended up in the earliest hours of the morning. The bar staff were rude and the drinks were stiff. It was one of the best places in the Quarter. "That sounds fantastic."

"*Laissez les bons temps rouler*," he said with a perfect Cajun accent.

Stacy smiled. *Let the good times roll*. And why not? It was her last night in New Orleans.

Ten exited the hotel and asked the bellman to hail him a cab. Dear God, but it was bright outside. He held up his hand to block out some of the light, but it didn't really work. He needed to get somewhere dark, cozy, where he could get some real sleep. While she had dozed peacefully in his arms, he had been awake most of the night, all too aware of her. He'd watched her sleep, which was admittedly a little weird, but he couldn't help himself. He loved holding her. He'd stayed awake as long as he could to enjoy every single last moment of every single one of her deep, steady breaths. The simple rise and fall of her chest while she lay in his arms was maybe the single most erotic thing ever. He didn't know when he had finally drifted off himself, but the next thing he knew, the alarm was blaring, and he was here, blinking in the sunlight.

The cab pulled up, and he rode up Magazine in a bleary-eyed haze. His suit was uncomfortable this morning after spending the whole night in it, but it still held her scent, and he hugged himself tightly to breathe her in again. The driver stopped at a traffic light, and happy, smiling couples crossed the street in front of the cab. He envied them the simple pleasure they had of spending that day with someone they loved.

He looked out the window, at the vibrant green trees, the white houses, the bright blue sky. New Orleans was a wonderful place, but it was not her place. He'd seen in her action last night. She'd come alive in that atmosphere, reveled in the games and competition. That was her soul, her passion, her life. And no matter how much he adored her, it was not something he could ever give her.

The cab came to a stop in front of his shop. He paid the driver, went inside, and called Joel to ask him to come in today and cover for him. The professor agreed as long as he could take Thursday off instead. Ten thought that sounded pretty reasonable.

He stuffed his phone back into his pocket and headed for his apartment. He ran his hand along the edge of the table at the back of the gallery as he passed it, the glossy finish smooth under his fingertips. He'd made the table when he'd bought the gallery, a place for the cash register and credit card machine to reside. Birds sang in the magnolia trees outside and dust motes danced in the beams of sunlight pouring in through the slatted window shades. He stopped, listening to the sounds of his home. He loved this place, the peace, the quiet, his solitary work. He'd put his heart and every dollar he had into getting it off the ground, and it had tested his belief in himself more than once. It was everything he had, and though that thought had once brought him what he believed to be happiness, right now all he felt was alone.

A police car zoomed down Magazine, lights and sirens blaring, and Ten rubbed his hand over his face. Sleep deprivation was making him loopy. He needed to get to bed. Exhausted, he went upstairs, stripped naked, and crawled under the covers.

He must have dreamed of her because when he awoke, she was glowing in his mind. He threw on some old jeans and a T-shirt and made some coffee. The color of her hair—the thought kept tickling the back of his brain. He'd spent much of the night memorizing the color and texture. Maybe now he could finally get that part right. He went to the painting and revaluated his work. Many things had to change.

He adjusted the canvas so it caught more of the late morning light and mixed up some paint. He needed to add a touch more red, like scarlet red, the red of lips and valentine's hearts. And then a bit of blonde, a hint of golden light. The contrast would create a richer image, something fuller, with more depth. Her hair had to be brighter at the top where the sunlight had hit her, but darker at the bottom, where the shadows in the room still clung to the night.

Hours later, the professor called up from the gallery, yelling something about a visitor. He frowned, torn between the painting and his own curiosity. He wasn't expecting anyone. The thought of simply not answering crossed his mind, but then Joel called again, and Ten sighed. He put the paints aside and went down to the shop to find out what was going on.

He heard her laughter before he saw her and when he opened the door to find Stacy smiling at Joel, his heart almost stopped. She was stunning, so beautiful she made him physically ache. She leaned over the counter to say something to Joel and the V-neck of her thin white T-shirt plunged a little lower, exposing a breathtaking view of the rounded curves of her breasts. From the seemingly strict way he kept his eyes on her face, he suspected the professor noticed as well.

Her face brightened when she made eye contact with him across the room. She gave him one of her outrageous smiles and he swore his knees went a little weak. "Hi."

"Hey," he replied, crossing the gallery to her side. He wrapped his arm around her waist, claiming her for himself. Her lips were parted, lush and glossy, and he dipped his head to steal a light kiss from her vanilla-flavored lips. "I thought you were going to text me?"

"I was," she said, smiling up at him. She gave him a little hug, a brief, sideways squeeze. "But I decided to walk instead. It's nice out. And it's been a long time since I've seen St. Charles Avenue."

Ten frowned. "Stacy, you shouldn't be walking alone—"

She held up her hand, cutting him off. "I used to live here, Ten. I'm not an idiot."

That was a can of worms he didn't dare open. "Okay, why don't you come on upstairs? I need to change and then we'll go to dinner."

"Sounds like a plan," she said.

"I'll lock up everything down here," Joel said. He smiled at Stacy. "It was nice meeting you."

She smiled back. "Have a great night, Joel."

"See you Saturday," Ten said and then escorted her through the door at the back of the shop leading up to his apartment. "Did you have a nice chat with Joel?"

"I did," she said with a grin. "He's an interesting guy."

"He isn't that interesting," he grumbled as he opened the door for her.

She laughed at his faked jealousy, which wasn't all that fake. "You know that he wants to own a gallery too, right? He has some really great ideas."

"I bet he does. Joel's a smart guy." They crossed the threshold and Ten was glad the back of the painting faced the entrance. He didn't want her to see it yet, not when it was unfinished and imperfect. He didn't want her to see how badly he'd failed. Because he had. He had nowhere near captured her beauty.

"Wow," she said looking around the wide open space. When he moved in, he had gutted the entire second floor, so that it was one, enormous space. His work area took up the entire right front part of the house, directly above the gallery, where it got the most light from the windows on both sides of the house. The kitchen was farther in, off to the left with a small table and chair set, his bed in the far back corner. The only doors in the place were for the bathroom and the closets. She spun around taking it all in. "Nice."

"I like it."

"Now, if that's the studio," she said, pointing to his workspace. "Then this must be the new bed." She crossed the room to look at it. He watched her fingertips move over the mahogany frame, tracing the intricate lines he had painstakingly carved with a chisel. "This is very nice."

"Thanks," he said, leaning against the closet door, directly opposite from where she stood. "I built it myself."

"You're pretty good with your hands, aren't you? Rebuilt your bike, the bed, you paint. What else do you?"

"I give pretty good massages too."

She smiled. "Yes, you do." She crossed over to him, reached up, touched his face, then showed him her red-stained fingertips. "Are you always covered in paint?"

"Yeah, usually." She was so close, he could smell her perfume, the clean scent of her shampoo. His body responded to her nearness, becoming hot and tight all over.

"These clothes are a mess." She traced the line of his collarbone, leaving behind a new smear of paint on his already stained shirt. "You should probably take them off."

His body temperature shot up about a thousand degrees, his blood sizzling through his veins. "Am I too dirty for you?"

She nodded slowly, her eyes fixed on his lips. "Yes, you're positively filthy."

Every bit of his heart was filled with longing for her. She was just exquisite. Smart, bold, beautiful. He'd never met a more desirable woman. He just wished he could show her how much she meant to him, how much he loved her.

The thought rebounded in his head, stopping his breath. Whoa. Full stop. What was that?

"Hey," Stacy asked. "Everything okay?"

"Yeah," he said absently, but he wasn't. He was all shook up. He tried out the words again in his head. He loved her. He shivered. That felt pretty good.

"Are you sure?" She stood on her tiptoes to look into his face. "You look a little pale."

He looked at her and smiled. *I love you.* A delightful tremor ran down his spine. "I'm okay. I just realized something I should've already known."

She furrowed her eyebrows, but there was a smile on her face. "What?"

He shook his head. "Nothing." His heart was beating too fast. He took her into his arms and pulled her against him.

"Hey," she said, making a very poor effort to push him away. "You're going to get me dirty too."

He hugged her tight and nipped her throat. "Don't worry. You'll be naked soon enough."

The smile that he loved so much was on her face when he kissed her. He caught her bottom lip between his teeth and tugged until she opened up and let him in. When her lips parted for him, he touched his tongue to hers. She moaned and his knees trembled, his raw need making him quake.

She pulled on the bottom of his shirt and he let her lift it off him, over his head. He sighed when she caressed his chest, her short fingernails scraping lightly again his skin. He cupped her breast through her shirt, the weight so familiar, but still new, outstanding and deeply arousing. She met his mouth for a hard kiss, telling him how much she liked his touch with her lips and tongue and teeth. She gasped when he reached under her shirt to touch her skin and when she moaned again, she set his entire world on fire.

She pulled away, lifted her shirt off, tossed it aside. He looked down at her breasts, admiring the curve of cleavage and all that was still hidden by her bra. He traced the top line of her breast, her skin hot under his fingertips. Her heart beat hard under his hand as he followed the line of her breast, memorizing every contour and curve. Every inch of her was burned into his memory, right along with the texture of her skin.

His hand slid to the back of her head, pulling her against him, holding her tight. Her body molded to his, fitting perfectly in his arms. She ran her hands down his back, exploring the muscles, then snaked around the front to caress his abs. When her hands rested on his belt buckle, he nearly lost his mind.

"I want you so much," he whispered, gripping her hair in his fists.

He lost all the air in his lungs when she cupped him, the electric thrill of her touch shooting up his spine. She looked up at him and smiled. He didn't think he'd ever been more aroused in his whole life. "How much?"

Her touch took him beyond any form of control. He was taken by his hunger, panting as he unzipped her pants, his heart pounding in his chest when he pushed them down. He didn't even know she was undoing his belt until he felt cool air on his skin and his pants fell down around his ankles.

She unfastened her bra herself, and he lost all that was left of his mind when she was fully naked before him. He knew she was beautiful, but that memory paled in the reality of seeing her now, again. He gaped at her, totally undone.

"What?" she asked a little shyly.

He tried to memorize every part of her face, her eyes, her lips, the dilation of her pupils. How was he ever going to do her justice? "You take my breath away."

She blushed at the compliment, her cheeks rosy. This was the woman he loved. The woman he wanted to be with forever. It could never really be, but they had tonight.

He took her into his arms and guided her to his bed. They laid down together, side by side, and breathed in each other's air. Slow, hesitant explorations became feverish as his need rose right along with the fire in his blood.

She gasped when he moved his hand lower, relishing her heat against his palm. He dipped his finger into her hot arousal, and she moaned into his ear, bucking against his hand, her eyes becoming glassy. He watched her pleasure build on her face, watched her whimper and writhe as he took her higher, bringing her to the edge and then toppling her over it, giving her every bit of pleasure he could strum out of her. She trembled when she came, her fingers digging into his wrist, as she moaned out a release so amazing, it vibrated in his very soul.

His need for her was throbbing, bordering on insane. He kissed her once, hard, and then reached over to get a condom from the nightstand. His fingers trembled as he tried to get the package open and he grunted in frustration when he failed.

"Here," she said, placing her hand over his. "Let me."

He could only watch stupidly as she opened the package, too drunk with his own desire to protest or move. She took the condom out and rolled it on to him. Once it was secured, he grabbed her for a long, deep kiss. He rolled on top of her, and her thighs automatically wrapped around his waist. He lifted her knee a little higher and slid into her heat with an eye-rolling moan.

He moved slowly at first, letting her get used to him, to the feel of their bodies joined. She gasped softly in his ear, moaning along with every thrust. His head fell to her shoulder, and he breathed in her hair, her skin, her scent. He wrapped his arms tightly around her and went deeper.

She rocked her hips and he picked up her rhythm, moving in time with her. She was everything to him, everything he ever wanted or needed, and when he kissed her, he hoped she felt how much she meant to him. How much he loved her.

Her fingers dug into his ass, painfully, erotically, and he increased the pace, obeying her silent command of more. He met her lips for another deep kiss, but she broke away with a cry when she found her release again. Her shudders and moans took him over the cliff, and he followed along after her, grunting out his pleasure as he exploded into her.

He held onto her for a long time, gripped her as he tried to come back to himself. He rolled onto his back, taking her with him, keeping her against his chest.

They held each other closely, tangled in the sheets and sweaty from their love. Early evening light filtered in the through the window over his bed, and he kissed her temple. He wished somehow that this night could be endless, that the morning would never come.

"I have to arrange a conference call as soon as I get back home tomorrow," she said, shifting in his arms.

He winced, unhappy with the reality check. "Thinking about work already, huh?" he asked, trying to keep his voice light.

He could feel her smile against his shoulder. "Always."

"Is that all you do in New York? Work?"

She sat up a bit, propping herself up on his chest. "Pretty much."

He traced the curve of her spine. "Don't you want anything else?"

"Of course. I want a family and everything. I just haven't met the right person yet."

He hated to know, he knew it could never be him, but he had to ask. "What would make him the right person?"

"I'd want someone who had a good job, who had lots of ambition. That way he'd understand when I worked late because his goals would be the same. Someone who could be charming at cocktail parties, but not want to go out every night. Someone who reads, who has opinions, who likes to go to free concerts in the park. Someone who wants a family, but not yet. Someone who focuses his on career and has the ability to succeed."

Yeah, he could scratch himself right off that list. "That's a lot of conditions."

"You know me. I know what I want." She drew patterns his chest, slow, lazy circles that made his skin prickle. "What do you want, Ten?"

He breathed in her scent, trying to absorb her very essence. "I think I just want to be in love."

She laughed, shook her head. "Whatever. You say that, and it's a nice thought, but how happy would you be if the woman you wanted to be with didn't let you have the time to paint?"

He frowned. "I wouldn't date someone who didn't."

"Exactly. And what about your bike? What if she hated your Harley?"

"I wouldn't know anyone that hated my bike."

"Huh-uh." She met his gaze. "We all have conditions."

He wanted to argue, but words died on his tongue. There was nothing he could say. She was right. He gathered her closer and kissed her instead.

Stacy woke up needing to pee. She wanted to stay in bed with Ten, warm and safe, but the need would not be denied. Resigned, she slipped out his arms and padded across the cool wood floor on bare feet.

They had forgone dinner, forgone everything to stay in bed, just talking and laughing and making love. She could still feel him inside her, feel how deeply he filled her. She was smiling when entered the bathroom, smiling when she came out. She suspected she was going to be smiling for days—the afterglow was that potent.

She crept back across the room to the bed. To him. She couldn't wait to crawl back in beside him, be enveloped in his arms, and snuggle against his chest. Listen to the sound of his heart and kiss the hollow of his throat, that little dip that was just made for her lips and always made him gasp. Hearing him gasp was the sexiest thing in the world, right up there with seeing him smile. Her gaze traced his sleeping form. His toes peeked out from under the sheet, his head buried somewhere in the pillows at the head of the bed. Pure, unabashed love for him rolled over her, warming her heart.

She froze in place, her eyes widening in the darkness. What was that feeling? Definitely not love. There was no way it could be that. Because if it was, that would open up a shitload of problems she absolutely did not want to deal with. Because if she loved him, that might change everything.

She turned away from the bed, away from him and the confusing things she did not want to want. Her gaze fell upon the canvas in the center of his studio, its back to her. The easel stood in a shaft of moonlight, and something about it was very enticing. It seemed to call to her, beckoning to her across the distance. She wanted to know want he was painting. She gave the bed a quick glance, saw that he was still sleeping, and circled around the easel to take a look.

She blinked once, twice, processing and yet not quite understanding all that she saw. It was a stunning painting, in hues of pink and cream and white and red, a hazy portrait of a woman sitting on a bed. Her face was indistinct, but she was achingly beautiful, the smile on her face both sad and happy, filled with longing and regret. She could feel the woman's desire, knew her heartbreak, and the love. Of course she could. That woman was her.

"*Her Perfect Lips*," Ten said.

She turned to find him standing a few feet away, naked in the moonlight. The look on his face reflected every raw, brutal, exquisitely gut-wrenching emotion coursing through her heart. She couldn't speak, too overwhelmed to respond. Because right in that moment, she was desperately, hopelessly in love with him and if she spoke, she might break down and confess something she would regret.

"*Her Perfect Lips*—that's what she's called," he went on, closing the distance between them. "It's from the last line of the Tennyson poem, *Sir Launcelot and Queen Guinevere*."

She knew the legend, but not the poem. "I'm not familiar with it."

He smiled. "*A man had given all other bliss, And all his worldly worth for this, To waste his whole heart in one kiss, Upon her perfect lips.*" He looked toward the painting. "She's not quite finished yet."

She didn't know what to say. She didn't know if there was anything she could say. "I didn't think you liked Tennyson's work."

A quick smile flashed across his handsome face. "I don't. Too depressing. But this one seemed appropriate."

She looked back at the painting. "She's beautiful."

His eyes flicked to the painting and then back to her. "Yes, you are."

She just shook her head. There were no words.

He reached toward the painting, brushing the air about a millimeter above the canvas. "I just can't seem to get it totally right. I thought I had captured you, but when I saw you again, I realized how wrong I was. I didn't even come close to capturing how truly beautiful you are. And so I worked on it some more. I want to get it right."

She looked to the painting and back to him. Here was her chance for something with him. Her chance to have the one thing she couldn't quite seem to achieve in New York. This was the moment to decide everything and change her future, her life.

"Don't go," he breathed out, raw emotion making his voice deep and husky.

Her eyes fell away from his. What was she thinking? It could never work. They wanted different things. She didn't belong in New Orleans any more than he belonged in New York. "I have to."

He nodded and it shredded her soul. It was the worst kind of déjà vu all over again. She was always right here with him, on the verge of something great, but unattainable. And though she knew what his answer was going to be, she said the words screaming in her heart anyway. "Come with me."

Her own struggle was reflected on his face. Finally, he shook his head. "I can't."

And there it was. The only answer they ever had for each other. She opened her arms to him, and he stepped into her embrace. She held him, his body pressed to hers, and she cupped his face in her hand. Stubble tickled her palm and she ran her thumb over his bottom lip. She'd never been sadder in her entire life. "Make love with me."

He took her mouth in a deep kiss that made her toes curl and set every one of her cells on fire. She let him back her up against the wall, let him lift her legs around his waist and take her weight. He gripped her hips hard and she cried out when he thrust into her, her fingernails digging into his shoulders. She squeezed him within her, then met his hips for every deep thrust. He watched her face, a smile playing on his lips as he pulled back and then plunged in again, making her groan.

Her head fell back against the wall and she gripped his firm ass for better leverage. She ground against him, needing him more. "Again."

He nipped her bottom lip hard and did as she asked, pulling out, and then thrusting back in deep.

His breath was hot on her throat where he licked and bit her, showering her skin with pleasure and sharp, thrilling pain. She wrapped her arms around him, holding on tightly as he increased the pace. She was panting now, sweating, the slap of their bodies and sound of their breathing loud in the quiet night.

She cried out when he pulled away, but before she could think, he spun her around, her cheek pressed against the cool wall. His erection pressed against her entrance and she arched her back, wanting him back inside her.

He teased her a little, barely dipping into her and then pulling away, driving her mad with desire. He leaned over her, his chest against her back, his lips to her ear. "What do you want?"

She cried out when he pressed the spot that made her whole body quake, turned her legs to liquid and her insides hum.

He bit down lightly on her shoulder, the scratch of his teeth against her flesh. "I can't hear you," he whispered in her ear.

She sucked in a deep, shuddering breath. "I want you."

He kissed her shoulder blade, the feel of him against her entrance so tormentingly sweet. "I asked you a question."

She was throbbing for him, needy, wet, and hot. "You!" she cried. "Oh, Ten, I want *you!*"

"Like this?" he asked.

She exhaled a long moan as he slowly, ever so slowly, filled her.

His lips whispered over her back, his breath cascading down her spine as the rhythm took them both away, carrying them beyond thought, taking them to mindless, incredible pleasure. She moaned with every thrust, going higher and higher with him. When he found his release, she came along with him, crying out through clenched teeth as the orgasm racked her being.

Lights flashed over the room as outside a car drove down Magazine. Ten's face was buried in her hair, the warmth of his breath on her neck.

"I love you, Stacy," he said.

Everything in her froze as emotion tore through her, rendering her immobilized. Her heart shattered, and she closed her eyes, resting her forehead against the wall. She wanted to scream *I love you too!* but there was no point in saying words that could never mean anything. "Please don't, Ten."

He spun her around to face him. "I know you're leaving. I know this is the end for us. But I wanted you to know that before you left. I love you, and I always have."

She touched his face, then looked away. Wasn't love supposed to conquer all? Why wasn't it this time? Was it all a lie? "Even if I felt the same—nothing would change. I'm still leaving tomorrow."

"I know. This isn't about anything other than letting you know. I'm not trying to get you to stay." He held her gaze. "I love you, and I want you to know. That's all."

His courage shamed her, made her realize how weak she had

been to try to keep her feelings from him. He deserved to know, and she owed it to herself to tell him—even though it changed nothing. "I love you, too."

"Don't say it if you don't mean it. I don't want that."

"I mean it," she said. "But it doesn't matter."

He hugged her fiercely. "It matters to me."

He lifted her up into his arms and carried her back to his bed. She breathed in his scent, licked his skin to memorize the texture and taste of him. She looked over his shoulder and watched the painting fade away as they crossed the large room. She clung to him, holding on for dear life, because she knew it would be the last time she could.

Chapter Six

Never before in her life had work ever been such an arduous task. Even just the simple act of getting out of bed every day required tremendous effort. She soldiered on though because she had to, because she refused to give in to the maudlin grief and tears that threatened to overwhelm her whenever she accidently thought about him. She went through her normal routine — wake up, coffee, shower, dress, walk, coffee, meeting, computer, lunch, computer, coffee, phone, home, dinner, bed—and felt about as alive as a Walking Dead extra. But it was only discipline that was going to get her through the heartache, not wailing away in the corner like some kind of demented banshee.

A lot of her problems stemmed from her own overactive imagination. Every night before she went to sleep, she imagined that Ten had come to the airport for her. She imagined different ways for him to have done it, sometimes she thought maybe because his love was so strong and glowing, the security agents would let him pass without a ticket to claim his one true love, or perhaps he charmed a female attendant, telling her he needed to propose to the love of his life, and the woman, a diehard romance fan, had let him through. Regardless of whatever reasons she made up, the fantasy always ended with him rushing into the lounge, taking her into his arms, kissing her madly, and then carrying her off to his place, where the real heat kicked in.

It was nice to think about, and it certainly warmed up her lonely bed, but it was making everything worse. She was holding on to something that didn't exist—a pretty lie she told herself because it was romantic and fun. Because the real truth of the matter was, even if he had shown up at the airport, she still would have gotten on that plane.

But that's not the way the story was supposed to go, was it? She told him she loved him. He loved her. Wasn't that supposed to fix everything? Wasn't that supposed to matter? Why were they apart?

Frustrated with herself, she got up from her desk and walked down the long second floor hallway of the Sharpe Designs offices toward the break room. The converted brownstone was a hive of silent activity, and she passed people tapping away at computer keyboards, creating and developing web sites, ad campaigns, media kits. This was the life she wanted, the one she had chosen. This was everything she worked for, everything she dreamed about. If only she could make herself believe it again.

She entered the break room, a large, cheerful space painted bright red, with tables and chairs, a coffee machine, water cooler, refrigerator, microwave. She wasn't hungry, but she got her lunch out of the fridge anyway and sat down toward the back of the room next to a window overlooking Spring Street. She watched the people down there, coming and going, living their lives.

She looked up as Dean Kirkwell entered the room. He was an attractive guy, the sexy boy-next-door, and though he was very taken, seeing him usually made her smile—but even that failed today. "Hey."

"Hey," he said, reaching into the refrigerator. He pulled out a container of milk and mixed together one of the protein shakes he seemed to be always drinking lately. Once he got the concoction stirred to his satisfaction, he gestured to the empty chair across from her. "This seat taken?"

"No, please, sit." It would be good to have company. She'd been alone in her own head for too long now, her thoughts swirling endlessly. Ten. New Orleans. New York. What she wanted from life. What she actually had. She welcomed the distraction.

He sat down and took a sip from his mug. "How's the new job treating you?"

"I love it." And she did. Every bit of it. It was also the only thing keeping her remotely sane. "Are you and Kat making beautiful blond babies yet?"

His smile grew wider and he shook his head. "Not yet, but it may be on a future agenda."

She returned his smile. At least someone was happy.

A man from facilities entered the room, emptied the trash, then left. Dean took a sip of his protein shake and Stacy grimaced. "Do you actually like those things?"

He shrugged. "They're all right. I'm thinking about doing the marathon again, and if I want to do that, I have to start training now."

"What does Kat think about that?" she asked, teasing him a little.

"Kat has promised to do very creative and very unpleasant things to me if I wake her up at four a.m. again to go running."

Stacy laughed. It felt good. She didn't think she'd laughed since she'd gotten back. "That does sounds like your girlfriend."

"Yes," he agreed. "The love of my life."

The mention of love made her heart hurt, and she winced, looking down at the table.

Dean studied her for long moment. "Is everything all right, Stace?"

She lifted her head to meet his gaze. "Yeah, why?"

"I don't know. You've been kind of quiet lately."

She nodded. There was no use in denying. She was usually the bubbly girl, always ready for something fun. She knew people had noticed the change. "Maybe I have been."

"Did everything go okay in New Orleans?"

"It was great." It was leaving that sucked. "I met a lot of people."

Ten. "Made some great connections."

He nodded slowly. "Okay."

They sat quietly together. Dean drank his potion while she pushed her tofu around on her plate. She should have packed something different today. Something spicy or maybe just warm. She could use some warmth right about now. She placed the food aside and looked out the window. "Have you ever done anything crazy, Dean?"

"Yes," he said.

"Like so crazy, you were afraid you might destroy everything you ever worked for, but you did it anyway?"

He nodded. "Yes."

Maybe he had. She wanted to believe him. She needed some outside advice because obsessing about in it her head obviously was not helping or working. "Let me ask you a question. Say, you and Kat met at a convention. Would you leave New York for her?"

He blinked, then tilted his head to the side as he thought it over. "If we just met at a convention…" He shook his head. "No, I doubt it. I mean, we'd barely know each other."

"Okay, well, say that you had a bit of history. That you ran into one another at a convention after a few years of losing touch. Would that make a difference?"

Dean raised an eyebrow. "How much history?"

Heat rose to her cheeks. "Some."

"Uh-huh," he said, smiling at her over his mug. "I assume we… reconnected?"

She blushed hard, and she just knew her face was as red as her hair. "Yeah."

He chuckled. "I see."

She waved away his amusement and leaned over the table toward him. "Would you do it? Would you leave New York for her?"

He sat back in the seat, exhaled a long breath and looked at the ceiling while he gave her question some thought. After a moment, he met her eyes again. "No, probably not."

His response was like a punch in the gut. There it was. The sad, hard truth. She'd made the right decision. Why did it feel so wrong? "You'd just let it go?"

"Well, maybe not that either. History is a powerful thing, and I do like Kat a lot. I've never done a long-distance relationship, but I might be willing to try it for her."

"Yeah, but wouldn't you want to be with her every day?"

"Sure. But since it had been years since we'd seen each other, we would need the time to get to know each other again. Relocation is huge. I'd want to be sure first."

She pressed her palms to the table, desperate for answers to the thoughts that had been plaguing her sleep. "But how would you work it out? Fly down Friday night, come back Monday morning? Spend a fortune in airfare for only a few hours together?"

"Maybe for a little while and probably not every weekend. She could come here too, you know." He took another drink. "She wouldn't consider moving?"

"She has a life too."

He nodded and was quiet for a while. "Sometimes you have to just go for it, Stacy. Even if you don't know what the outcome is going to be. Even if it's not exactly what you thought you wanted. Some things are just worth trying."

She thought about all her plans. The dream she had of her perfect life. Ten did not fit into any of that. And she didn't want to make him fit into either. She liked him just the way he was. "But what if it's not what I want?"

Dean held her gaze. "What if it is?"

***

Ten stood in front of the painting, watching the early morning sunlight adding shadows and depth to the canvas. He saw every flaw, every mistake, everything he'd got wrong. It was an insurmountable task. Every time he worked on it, he risked ruining it.

Every time he picked up a paintbrush, he only made it worse. He couldn't do it. He'd never be able to do her justice. He lacked the talent, the vision—the heart.

He sighed and looked away from the painting and his failure. This apartment offered no solace. It had probably been a week since he'd swept, and he could see traces of dirt on the hardwood floor. A little green lizard skittered across the windowsill, then dropped out of sight. His laundry piles were growing out of control. That was something he could fix. All he needed to was call Hula Mae's and they would come, take his clothes away, wash them, fold them, and return them to him in a neat pile. Outside light flickered across the painting, catching his eye. Ten could only shake his head. The woman he loved had left him and he was all jacked-up about laundry. Pathetic.

He scrubbed his face in his hands and tried to find some semblance of balance. He'd told her he loved her for god's sake. And he'd meant it with all his heart. Why didn't that mean something? Why were they apart?

He tormented himself with questions, but he already knew the answers. Words without action were meaningless, no matter how heartfelt. If he wanted her as badly as he sat around and thought he did, then he needed to do something about it, take some kind of decisive action for once in his life. He looked at his phone and then away. Then he looked at it again, got up off the stool, and called Joel.

In the span of a single ring, he regretted his hastiness, not wanting to make the decision he had come to days and days ago. In his head, it all made perfect sense, and everything turned out happily-ever-after, but actually putting it into action was a huge risk. There were so many factors he couldn't control, so many *what ifs.*

He stared at the painting and when Joel answered, Ten took a deep breath and said, "Hello."

"What's up?" Joel asked.

Did he really want to do this? *Could* he do this? Yes, he had to. "Can you stop in sometime today? There's something I want to ask you."

"Something wrong, Ten?"

Yes. Everything. "Nah, man, I just want to ask you something. It's good. I promise."

"All right." Joel said, but Ten could hear the hesitation in his voice. "I'll be there in about an hour."

"Great. I'll be upstairs. Come on up."

He could almost feel Joel's shock. "You're not opening the store today?"

"Later. I need to talk you to first."

There was a long pause. "Are you sure everything's all right?"

"I think it's going to be."

He hung up the phone, poured himself some coffee, and sat back down in front of the painting. Even its title seemed to mock him, the last passage of the poem asking him what he was willing to do for her kiss. He touched her lips, the smile he could never get right, and decided he was going to risk it all for something she might not even want.

Joel arrived twenty minutes later, a bundle of nervous energy. "What's up, Ten?" he asked as soon as he walked in.

"Relax," Ten said, getting up from the stool to greet the other man. "Would you like some coffee?"

"Sure," Joel said, following him to the kitchen.

Ten poured him a mug and they sat down at the table. He stared into his coffee, trying to muster the strength. This was it. If he was going to do it, he had to do it now. "How would you feel about buying the gallery?"

Joel blinked. "Repeat that for me, please?"

Ten took a deep breath. He had to take this slowly. He didn't want to scare Joel off. "I'm going to be traveling soon. I'd like you to have the shop."

Joel leaned back in the chair and exhaled a hard breath. "This is not what I expected. I thought you were going to tell me you were closing the gallery and I was out of a job."

Ten's gaze traveled over his apartment, the cream walls and scattered canvasses, the paint-splattered hardwood floor, his unmade bed. He was going to miss it. "I'd rather you had it. I love this place. I'd like to see it go on."

Joel nodded slowly, and Ten held his breath. Everything relied upon this answer. The silence stretched out and Ten listened to sound of his own nervous heart. His breath caught when Joel finally met his eyes again. "No."

"What?" he blurred out, too flabbergasted for any real, coherent reply.

"No," Joel repeated, shaking his head for emphasis. "I don't want to buy the gallery."

Ten's stomach took a nauseating plunge. There went all his dreams, his big plans and fantasies. Without the capital from the sale of the gallery, he'd never be able to get a decent start in New York.

"What I would like," Joel went on, "is a partner."

Joel was speaking, but the words were not penetrating through Ten's dismay. "What?" he asked again, feeling more than a little stupid.

"A partnership," Joel said. "I'd like to own the gallery with you."

Ten shook his head. "I'm leaving New Orleans."

"I get what you're doing, Ten, but maybe it isn't the wisest course of action. Maybe all you need to do right now is work on getting this place a decent website."

The possibility hit him in the gut. Could he have both the gallery and the woman he loved? It would be difficult commuting back and forth to New York, and he wouldn't be able to see her as much as he wanted to, but maybe that was what they needed. Time to get to know one another. For the first time since she left, he felt real hope. He met Joel's gaze. "Maybe we could use a whole new marketing plan."

Joel smiled. "I agree." He glanced around the apartment. "Besides, I wouldn't want to live up here. I've found that most women prefer men who have places with actual rooms, and you know, furniture."

Shock made Ten's eyebrows rise. "I have furniture."

Joel gave him a dry look. "Tennyson, a bed, two chairs, a table, and a stool do not count as furniture."

Ten laughed. God, it felt good. "What do you know about women anyway?"

"I know that they don't like to be kept waiting." He grinned at Ten. "When are you leaving?"

"Wow, I don't know. I wanted to talk to you first." He'd been so worried about Joel's answer, he'd hadn't thought any further ahead. Joy made his head feel light and warmth filled his chest. He was going to New York. He was going to see her. "Soon. As soon as I can."

"Good," Joel said, rising to his feet. He held out his hand. "We're going to make a hell of a team."

"Yeah," Ten said, taking Joel's hand. "I agree. I'll talk to my lawyer and we'll figure out what needs to be done, find out what kind of paperwork we'll need."

He gestured toward the apartment door and walked Joel downstairs to the front of the shop. He unlocked the door and held it open.

Joel hesitated for a second. "You're making a good choice, Ten. She's worth it."

An edge of nerves shot though Ten's composure, but he quickly suppressed it. He was right. She was worth it. "Yeah, I think so."

Joel smiled. "Okay. Tell her hi for me when you see her."

Ten shook his head. "No, I will not." He pointed to the door. "Get out."

Joel laughed, and Ten laughed along with him. They said their goodbyes, and he closed the door behind the professor. He exhaled hard. The first step was a success. Now the real work kicked in. If he wanted her, he needed to go to New York and work something out with her. There had to be a way for them to meet at least halfway, to develop some kind of arrangement. He was willing to travel, willing to compromise his time to be with her all that he could. He'd told her he loved her. Those words carried some responsibility, and if he wanted them to mean anything at all then he had to prove it.

He just hoped she was willing to do the same.

Chapter Seven

Ten's contact information was showing on her phone, the little icons on the screen offering her the option of texting or calling him. She tapped her nail against the edge of the case. What would she say? There really wasn't anything to say. Hi? How's it going? I love you desperately, please, please come see me? I can't live without you? Nothing with a point. She put the phone aside and looked back at the spreadsheet on her computer screen, taking her time to update the progress reports on the various alternative social media venues she and her staff had explored since she returned from the conference. Many of them had turned out to be not right for Sharpe Designs for one reason or another, but they were successfully using a small international networking site that worked like a kind of hybrid secret lovechild of Twitter and Facebook. They had a number of engaged followers already and had even managed to pick up a new client in Vienna—all within the first two weeks of implementation. Martin Padgett had given her some good advice, and she couldn't wait to tell him about her success the next time she spoke with him.

A couple of her coworkers came laughing down the hallway, and she overheard them talking about where they were going to go have drinks. The whole office was buzzing with Friday fever, but Stacy wasn't into it. She had no plans for the weekend. She could have some if she wanted to, she could go out with any number of her coworkers tonight, or she could go to movie, see a show, check out her online dating email and see if anyone interesting had written to her. She had a million options. She was young and free and in the heart of New York City, but not one single thing appealed to her because all she really wanted was Ten.

She picked up her phone again, her thumb hovering over the text icon on the screen. Why did she hesitate? She had never failed in the past to go for exactly what she wanted. She wanted Ten. Simple. The problem was, having him would alter her entire life plan. Ten didn't fit into her strict idea of success.

She pressed the little green icon, her heart racing as she brought up her contacts and choose his name from the list. Foolish. Stupid. Pointless. It was only going to cause more heartache. But she yearned to talk with him, to hear his voice, his laughter. What she really wanted was to feel his warmth again, taste his lips, drown in the pleasure of his caress, but tonight, right now, it would be enough to just sit and chat and laugh with him. Any little contact would help soothe the constant pain in her chest. It had to, nothing else was working. Her thumbs trembled slightly as she typed, "I miss you."

She stared at the words on the screen for a long time. Her thoughts went far away, lost in the memories of their last night together. Making love with him had been outrageous, but afterwards was really special. The time they spent in each other's arms, kissing, touching, exploring, and talking softly in the darkest hours of the night. It was insane how acutely lonely she was without him. She never realized what a solitary life she led. Without him, it felt like the best part of her was missing, like she was only half the person she was before. She wanted her good husband back.

Her email pinged, but she ignored it. The question she'd been tormenting herself with for weeks circled in her head. Could she live without him? But she understood now that was the wrong question. Of course she could live without him. She'd done just fine for years and years without him. She wasn't so helpless that she'd cease to breathe or exist. The question she should be asking, the only one she really needed an answer to was: Did she want to?

She put her phone aside, the message unsent. A text was not the answer. Nothing short of crawling into his arms, holding him close, and never letting go was going to satisfy the hollow space in her heart. She had to see him again. They had to work something out. There had to be a way.

She turned to her computer and opened a Word document. *Dear Ron*, she typed and then stopped. Dear Ron, what? Dear Ron, I can't bear to live without this man in New Orleans, so I'm totally giving up on the one thing I thought I wanted most in life to go be with him? Oh, and by the way, I'm not even sure if he'll be happy about this decision since I haven't actually spoken to him since I left.

The curser blinked on the blank page, insistent and demanding. Her fingers hovered over the keyboard. Her instant messenger chimed, and for a second she thought about seeing what it was, forgetting about all this craziness, and getting some actual work done. But she knew if she let this moment pass her by, she was never going to get the courage up to do it again. It was now or never. She had to do something she had never done before in her life. She had to take a risk.

She was so tense that when her desk phone rang, she nearly jumped out of her skin. The display showed that Ron was calling her from his office and without any thought at all, she picked up the receiver. "Hello?"

"Stacy," Ron said, sounding as jovial as ever. "Will you come up to my office for a minute, please?"

"Okay," she answered, her stomach flipping over. Ron might be a great person, but it was never good to be called to your boss' office in the middle of the day. "I'll be right there."

She got up from her desk and headed upstairs. What could he want? She wasn't working on anything sensitive right now, and there was nothing she could think of that he'd need an update on.

She reached the top floor and took a left at Kat and Dean's alcove. Nobody was there, but she did see Alan when she passed by his glass office. She waved to him as she headed down the hall, her palms becoming clammier and clammier as she got closer to Ron's office.

Ron's assistant, Mary Ellen, was looking as chic as ever in a boldly diagonal stripe blouse with a wide collar. The older woman's white-blonde hair was coiffed to perfection and she looked like the sentry she was, guarding Ron's inner sanctum. Stacy greeted her with a smile, and Mary Ellen told her to go on back, that Ron was ready and waiting for her.

She pushed open the door to her boss' enormous office, stepped over the threshold, and lost every bit of breath in her lungs.

"Hey, Stacy," Ten said, looking up at her from one of Ron's comfortable guest chairs. He smiled, like none of this was surreal or even a very big deal.

She knew some kind of reply was probably required, but all she could do was gape. Her mouth hung open as took in every little detail, from the way his dark hair curled at the nape of his neck, the faded blue T-shirt that clung to the muscles in his arms and chest, the well-fitted jeans, and motorcycle boots. Seeing him was wonderful and terrible, and her system overloaded from the shock, joy, and confusion.

Ron cleared his throat and she blinked, trying desperately to pull herself together. He gave her a sympathetic smile and gestured for her to take the seat beside Ten. She crossed the room on legs that didn't feel quite real and numbly sat down.

"Tennyson has decided to hire us to redo his website," Ron said once she got settled. He looked at the computer screen where he had Ten's current website up and shook his head with mock sorrow. "A decision I wholeheartedly agree with."

She nodded, still too blown away to form a coherent thought. She couldn't keep her eyes off Ten. She wanted to touch him, hug him, kiss him, make sure he was actually there and not some cruel figment of her overactive imagination. She wanted to breathe in his scent, feel his warmth, but also maybe slap him around a little bit. Why hadn't he called her?

"I think we can do great things for Tennyson, don't you agree, Stacy?"

She tore her gaze away from Ten with some reluctance and met Ron's eyes. "Absolutely."

"I'm going to assign our best team to it right away Tennyson, but the reason I called you in, Stacy, was as we were talking, an idea occurred to me that I'd like to bounce off the two of you," Ron went on. "Stacy, did you read the article in *AdVantage* magazine about a firm holding free symposiums for architects and interior designers, which would give them their required continuing education credits?"

She nodded, not sure where this was going. "I did. It sounded like pure advertising to me though. 'Sponsor' companies coming in to talk about "*How to work with this exciting new marble*," but really just pitching their products to a bribed audience."

"I thought the same thing, but it got me thinking that maybe we could do something similar. We represent a fair number of galleries and artists right now. I'd love for you to arrange a way for them to meet with one another and get a network event going." He turned to Ten. "Would you be interesting in attending a gathering of other gallery owners and artists? A networking event?"

Ten thought it over. "It depends. Is it a sales pitch? No matter who was attending, I don't think I'd go to something like that." He paused. "But if it was more a salon. I'd be interested in that."

Stacy brightened, ideas quickly coming to her. "Yes, like a literary salon. Something very loose and informal. Set up a ballroom, a bar with coffee, tea, beer, wine, light beverages. People could talk, mingle, share ideas, and network."

"Yeah, but how would that benefit you?" Ten asked. "The only thing artists like more than free drinks is bragging. And the more drinks they have…" He shook his head. "I don't see how you'd pitch your services effectively in that kind of environment."

She nodded, seeing his point. "Well, we'd have to direct the focus of the gathering in some way. Maybe have themes." She waved her hand as her thoughts raced. "I don't know, we choose to concentrate on something like—New Art Selling Trends. Whatever. We could invite experts to come in and mingle and talk. Hold an informal Q&A to encourage questions and discussions. We could offer information, advice…"

"And professional assistance," Ten said, smiling. "Yes, that could work. No hard sells though. Just an exchange of ideas and services."

"Yes," Stacy said smiling back. "And it would also be a great way for us to learn more about their needs and how we can do better business with them."

"I like it," Ron said. He turned to Ten. "Tennyson, is this something you'd be willing to help us launch? From what I'm hearing, it sounds like this project needs your direct input. We'd love to have you as an official consultant and perhaps we could do an exchange? Your new website package in return for your expertise? I think we'd only have to take you away from your life once a month for a few months until we got the kinks out. And eventually, I think we could do satellite salons in New Orleans and other cities as well."

Ten nodded slowly, considering Ron's offer. Stacy felt funny, dizzy and tense. Would he accept the offer? What would it mean if he didn't? What would it mean if he did?

He met Ron's gaze. "I'd love to."

She exhaled a breath she hadn't realized she had been holding. They were going to be working together again. She didn't know if she wanted to puke or explode with joy.

Ron smiled. "Fantastic. I think you and Stacy will work very well together. I have full confidence in your abilities." He tapped a few keys on the keyboard and studied whatever he'd called up on his screen. "Tennyson, I'm seeing here that Dean Kirkwell is not available until late Monday morning to meet with you. I truly believe he is the best man for your website and I'd love for you to work with him. Will you still be in town on Monday?"

Ten sat back in the chair, shot her a quick side-glance and then looked back at Ron. "I hope so."

"Excellent," Ron said, tapping a few more keys. "Stacy, I'd like you to spend time developing a rough outline of how you envision the salon working." He gave her a wide-eyed innocent look. "Perhaps you and Tennyson can get together over the weekend and discuss some of the details?"

Stacy's eyes narrowed. She'd heard about Ron and his love for matchmaking. This was beginning to feel a lot like a set up. "I think Ten and I can work something out."

"Wonderful," Ron said and stood up. Ten stood up as well and they shook hands. "Now if you'll excuse me, I have to go meet with Alan." He gave them both a big smile and then left them alone in his office.

Ten turned and looked at her. "What just happened?"

She shook her head, not really sure herself. She wanted to reach out and touch him, reassure herself that he was real. "I can't believe you're here."

"Stacy…" he began, then paused, shook his head. "You were right. I need a new website."

"Uh-huh," she said. "And what brought about this change?"

The afternoon sunlight streamed in through the windows, playing on his jaw, highlighting the light stubble on his cheeks. She'd dreamed of this, but now that it was happening she was unsure. If she went forward with him, it would change her entire life.

He nibbled his lower lip and her stomach did a little flip. "It was the painting."

She couldn't have heard that right. "The painting brought you here?"

"*Her Perfect Lips*. I look at it every day and I can't work on it. And it made me wonder what I was willing to do to be with you.

What would I sacrifice for just one kiss?" He met her gaze, his eyes drilling into hers. "I'm not that noble, but I don't want to live without you. Something had to change."

She rubbed her fingertips over her eyebrows, trying to process the feelings he inspired, the confusion and anxiety, the hope and love. He disordered her orderly life. It was unsettling and completely wonderful. "So, what do you have in mind?"

He shook his head. "I'm not really sure. But I want to discuss it with you." He leaned forward and placed his hand over hers. "I think we can find some way to be together." He held her gaze. "If that's something you want."

Stacy looked away from him, from the promise in his green eyes. This was exactly what she thought she wanted, exactly what she dreamed about, and it was terrifying. "How are we ever going to have a real relationship?"

"I don't know," he said. "But I think we should try."

This meant that she was not going to have a partner who she could wake up to every morning, couldn't live the dream of reading the Sunday paper with him in bed unless he happened to be in town, couldn't just call him up on the spur of the moment and have dinner because she was thinking of him and wanted to see him. Everything about this deal was going to be part time. She wasn't sure if it was going to be enough for her. "It's not going to be that easy, Ten."

He snorted. "Nothing ever is."

She wanted him. He was the only one she wanted. Just a minute ago, she had been willing to give up her whole life for him. Now she had a chance to be with him, a chance for a future. She had to go for it. No plans, no schemes, just a blind leap of faith. "I was thinking about you today."

He raised an eyebrow, a smile playing on his lips. "You were? What were you thinking about?"

She held his gaze. "I was thinking about going down to New Orleans to see you."

He was a quiet for a moment, absorbing what she said and all that was left unsaid. A hint of a grin flashed across his lips and he reached out to stroke her hair. "Was that all you were thinking about?"

She wanted to smile, to laugh, to confess everything she had ruminated on and then make him explore each and every one of those thoughts in minute detail, but she forced herself to keep a straight face. "Yeah, that was pretty much it."

He took her hand, laced his fingers though hers. "We can work this out, Stacy."

Her whole life changed with the simple nod of her head. "We'd better. Ron is expecting results."

He smiled, and she saw the relief in his handsome features. The hope. "I think he's expecting us to work very closely together."

She smiled. She could do this. "We already have an assignment for the weekend."

He nodded. "That's right. We do. It looks like I'll need a place to stay."

She ran her thumb over his knuckles. "I have chips at my place."

He grinned wickedly, stood up, and pulled her into a tight embrace. His body melded to hers, so familiar, comfortable, exciting. She thought maybe if he held her like this every time they were together, things might actually be okay. "Well, that settles that," he said, rocking her gently in his arms. "I really like chips."

9 780000 812346